Other books written by this author you may enjoy as well

Star Battles: The Valkyrie Saga Book:One "Rise of the Ascendancy"

(published by Trafford Publishing)

STAR
BATTLES

Uniform Recognition Manual of the Terran Imperial Forces

Kenneth Michael Hamblett

Order this book online at www.trafford.com
or email orders@trafford.com

Most Trafford titles are also available at major online book retailers.

© Copyright 2014 Kenneth Michael Hamblett.
All rights reserved. No part of this publication may be reproduced, stored in a retrieval
system, or transmitted, in any form or by any means, electronic, mechanical, photocopying,
recording, or otherwise, without the written prior permission of the author.

Printed in the United States of America.

ISBN: 978-1-4907-3486-6 (sc)
ISBN: 978-1-4907-3487-3 (hc)
ISBN: 978-1-4907-3488-0 (e)

Library of Congress Control Number: 2014908031

Because of the dynamic nature of the Internet, any web addresses or links contained in
this book may have changed since publication and may no longer be valid. The views
expressed in this work are solely those of the author and do not necessarily reflect the
views of the publisher, and the publisher hereby disclaims any responsibility for them.

Any people depicted in stock imagery provided by Thinkstock are models,
and such images are being used for illustrative purposes only.
Certain stock imagery © Thinkstock.

Trafford rev. 04/29/2014

Trafford
PUBLISHING®   www.trafford.com
North America & international
toll-free: 1 888 232 4444 (USA & Canada)
fax: 812 355 4082

Please note: While this book presents a lot of insignia and uniforms, this manual by no means shows every single insignia and uniform. For that, another volume would need to be written for that. I hope everyone enjoys this second book within the new Star Battles Universe.

DEDICATION

I dedicate this book to one of my best friends. She is like a sister and her name is Karen Duckett. I would like to also thank my best friend Michael Manton and his beautiful wife Marie. All three of these people are family to me. I love them all so very much!

INTRODUCTION

Hello recruits! Welcome to the Imperial Armed Forces of the greatest galactic nation to ever have existed. I am second in command of the Empire's military forces, and you may address me as Grand Admiral. Her highness the Queen of the Empire has a symbolic role. His or her Lordship/Ladyship the Supreme Chancellor has a supreme advisory role.

This manual will help the recruit to be able to quickly recognize the many insignia and uniforms of the Imperial Armed Forces of the mid-27th century. After reading this manual, you should be able to know upon sight your superiors and inferiors. The Imperial Armed Forces has an elaborate rank system, and many varieties of uniforms and insignia. The Imperator is the Supreme Commander of the Imperial Armed Forces. His or her official title as supreme commander is Commander-In-Chief.

Congratulations on your decision to help defend the Empire . . . Hail to the Empire!

Grand Admiral Xavier Noble

Office of the Grand Admiral

Terran Star Empire
Great Seal

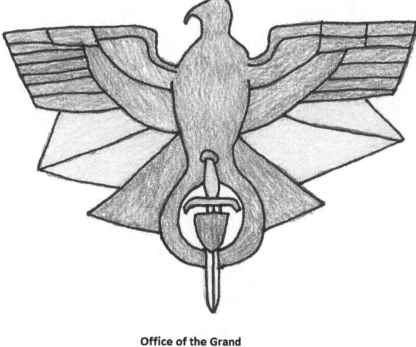

**Office of the Grand
Admiral**

Grand Military
Banner

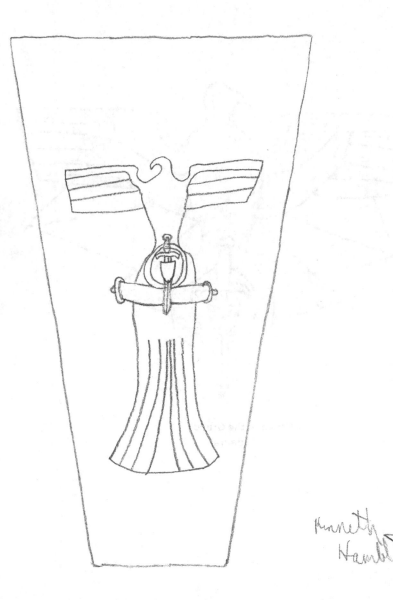

Imperial military Banner

Department of
War and Defense

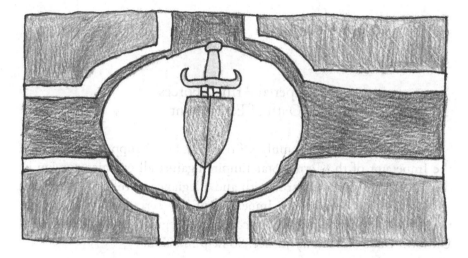

NATIONAL WAR FLAG

Imperial Armed Forces
Oath of Enlistment

I,(your name), do solemnly affirm that I will support and defend the Imperator of the Terran Star Empire against all enemies, foreign or domestic, that I will bear true faith and allegiance to the same; and that I will obey the orders of the Imperator of the Terran Star Empire and the officers appointed over me, according to regulations of the Imperial Uniform Code of Military Justice. So help me God.

CHAPTER ONE:
INSIGNIA

SECTION ONE:
Military Occupancy rating insignia

This section of the manual will show you not all, but some of the mos/rating insignia of the Imperial military forces. Your MOS or otherwise called rating, will signify the main "job" or what kind of soldier, marine, or sailor you are. MOS/Rating insignia are brass, except for the Nursing Corps. Their insignia is that of a red cross with white border. MOS/Rating insignia is the same for enlisted and commissioned officers, and are placed centered on each collar of standard service and dress uniforms.

Each MOS/Rating is known as a corps(pronounced as core). Each corps has a corps color. These colors are shown on epaulettes, some waist sashes, shoulder straps, and otherwise indicated. Both enlisted personnel and commissioned officers wear their primary corps color.

MOS/Rating colored stripes: These are at least 2 inches wide and placed on each side of regulation pants, shorts, skirts, and skorts. These colored stripes are for company-grade commissioned officers. Field-grade commissioned officers have colored stripes with silver edges. Flag-grade commissioned officers have colored stripes with gold edges.

Warrant Officers: They have a 2 inch wide silver stripe on each pants leg.

Chiefs-Of-Staff: Their stripes are like flag-grade officers, except an additional 1 cm wide gold stripe runs centered down middle of bigger stripe.

Supreme Admirals/Marshals: Are similar to the Chiefs-of-Staffs, except the stripes are red.

Grand Admiral: Are similar to Supreme Admirals and Marshals, but have 2 gold 1 cm stripes running down middle of bigger stripe placed 1 cm from edges.

Commander-in-Chief: Is the Same as Grand Admirals.

Military Occupancy Specialty Rating colors: not every MOS/Rating are covered in this volume, however, some are represented as follows . . .

white= starship commanders, Inspector General, Adjutant General

green= medical, nursing, and psychiatry services

light blue= infantry

dark blue= science corps

yellow= engineering, security, military police, judge advocate general's corps

crimson= ordnance, torpedoman corps

pink= communications, signal, and yeoman corps

brown= quartermaster and personnel corps

purple= pilots

red= artillery and gunners

gray= transportation corps

black= chaplain corps

orange= cavalry and tactical corps

Military occupancy specialty Insignia

1. Adjutant General's corps:
   MOS color~ white

2. Artillery corps:
   MOS color~ red

3. Pilot's corps:
   MOS color~ purple

4. Torpedoman corps:
   MOS color~ crimson

5. Gunner corps:
   MOS color~ red

6. Command corps:
   MOS color~ white

Military occupancy specialty Insignia

7. Finance corps:
   MOS color— Canary Yellow

8. Science corps:
   MOS color— blue

9. Tactical corps:
   MOS color— orange

10. Boatswain corps:
    MOS color— Yellow

11. Cryptologic Technician corps:
    MOS color— scarlet

12. Yeoman corps:
    MOS color— pink

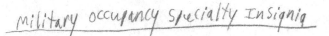

Military occupancy specialty Insignia

13. Engineering corps:
    MOS color~ yellow

14. communications corps:
    MOS color~ pink

15. Nursing corps:
    MOS color~ green

16. Psychiatry Corps:
    MOS color~ green

17. chaplain corps:
    MOS color~ black

christian   Jewish   Muslim

SECTION TWO:
Badges

Imperial Armed Forces Member Badge

This badge has two types and many variants. It's awarded to military personnel after graduation from basic combat training. The type and variant depends on the wearer's rank and uniform. This badge is placed 1/8th inch under the bottom row of ribbons. Type-1 consists of the Imperial Sword and Shield symbol. The shield is, of course, pointing downwards behind the shield. It is two inches long, 1 ½ inches wide.

Type-1 variants:
Junior cadets and midshipman is gold longsword with gold shield
Senior cadets and midshipmen has silver longsword with silver shield.
Enlisted soldiers/sailors/Non-commissioned officers/Warrant officers/Commissioned officers has gold longsword with silver shield

Type-2 variants:
Type-2 is similar to type-1, except the sword and shield are suspended by a colored ribbon. This type is worn by warrant officers and commissioned officers on dress uniforms as an optional item if they prefer wearing it over wearing type-1. The longsword is gold, while the shield is silver. The variants of this type are as follows . . .

Warrant officers(light gray ribbon)
Company-grade Commissioned officers(light blue ribbon)
Field-grade commissioned officers(purple ribbon)
Flag-grade commissioned officers(red ribbon)

Armed Forces Member Badge
~~Badge of Military Honor~~

* This badge has 2 types and many variants according to rank. It's awarded to military members after graduation from basic combat training. The type and variant that's worn depends on the wearer's rank. this badge is placed centered 1/8 inch under the bottom row of ribbons.

type-1: 2 inches long

type-2: gold long sword, silver shield
(2 in. long)

ribbon is 2 in. long

Variants-

A. cadet/midshipman
(gold longsword w/ gold shield)

B. Senior cadet/senior midshipman
(silver long sword w/ silver shield)

C. Enlisted soldiers and sailors and Non-Commissioned Officers
(gold long sword w/ silver shield)

A. warrant Officer variant (light grey ribbon)
B. company-Grade officer variant (light blue ribbon)
C. Field-Grade officer variant (purple ribbon)
D. Flag-Grade officer variant (red ribbon)

Service Star

The service stars denote how many years the wearer has served in the military. It's a five-pointed star pointing upwards. These are placed in rows of four left of the Imperial Armed Forces Member Badge. When officers are wearing the dress type of the IAFMB, these stars are placed left of the sword and shield part of the badge. The stars are ½ inch in diameter. Worn behind these stars is a colored plastic disk. The disk color depends on the wearer's branch. If a person transfers to another branch, the disk color of any service stars earned in the old branch stays the same. Service stars earned in the new branch will reflect the new branch's color.

Bronze star= 1 year
Silver star= 5 years
Gold star= 10 years

light blue disk= Army
black disk= Imperial Navy
green disk= Marine Corps
orange disk= Special Forces Operations Command
red disk= Imperial Storm Trooper Legions

Combat Star

The combat stars denote how many years the wearer has served in combat operations. It's a five-pointed star pointing upwards. The star is blood red in color with a colored border denoting the years. The star is ½ inch in diameter and is worn in rows of four right of the Imperial Armed Forces Badge. When officers are wearing the dress type of the IAMB, the stars are placed right of the sword and shield part of the badge.

Bronze border= 1 year
Silver border= 5 years
Gold border= 10 years

Squad Leader's Badge

This badge is a silver colored shield with a white, five-pointed star pointing up in the middle of the shield. The shield is pointed downwards. It is worn 1/8th inch above top row of ribbons.

Platoon Sergeant's Badge/
Platoon Petty Officer's Badge

This badge is similar to the Squad Leader's Badge, except with the addition of a silver longsword pointing downwards behind the shield.

Platoon Leader's Badge

This badge is similar to the Squad Leader's Badge, except with the edition of two silver crossed swords behind the shield.

Company Commander's Badge

This badge is similar to the Platoon Leader's Badge, except it is gold in color.

First Sergeant's Badge/
First Petty Officer's Badge

This badge is a silver-colored diamond 2 inches long, 2 inches wide, and is placed 1/8th inch above top row of ribbons. It also has a white, five-pointed star pointing upwards in the middle of the diamond.

Squad Leader's Badge

is silver in color and worn 1/8 inch above top row of ribbons, 2 inches long, 3 inches wide.

Platoon Leader's Badge

is silver in color and worn 1/8th inch above top row of ribbons, 2 inches long, 3 inches wide.

Platoon Sergeant's Badge/ Platoon Petty Officer's Badge

is silver in color and worn 1/8 inch above top row of ribbons, 2 inches long, 3 inches wide.

First Sergeant's Badge/First Petty Officer's Badge

is silver in color and worn 1/8 inch above top row of ribbons, 2 inches long, 3 inches wide.

Pilot's Qualification Badges

These badges consists of the Imperial Shield and Sword symbol, with wings attached to each side left and right of the shield. These badges are placed 1/8th inch above top row of ribbons. Starfighter pilots wear gold version of the badges, while all other craft pilots wear silver. The badge's wingspan is 3 inches wide. Squadron Leader's wings have a hollowed out circle(the circle must not have a diameter touching the wing tips, rather they go behind each mid point of each wing). Wing Commander's wings are like Squadron Leader's wings, except a gold or silver star is in the middle of the shield.

Starbase/Outpost Commander's Badge

This badge is gold-colored and placed 1/8th inch above top row of ribbons. The badge is 2 inches in diameter, and is a five-pointed star pointing upwards with a hollowed out circle behind star. Star points are longer than the circle.

Starship Commander's Badge

This badge is a gold-colored trident with a hollowed-out circle around the trident. The tips of the trident is longer than the circle. It is placed 1/8th inch above top row of ribbons. The badge is 2 inches in diameter.

Insignia

Pilot's wings

(gold for starfighters
silver for other craft)

Starbase / outpost commander's
Badge

is gold-colored and placed 1/8th inch above the
top row of ribbons. the badge is 2 inches in
diameter.

Squadron Leader's
wings

Starship commander's Badge

wing commander's
wings

SECTION THREE:
Service hat and dress hat insignia

Training Recruits

Basic training recruits wear a 2 inch-wide, 2 ½ inches long Imperial Shield insignia on their service hats and dress hats. It's made out of brass. It has a cm-in diameter circle raised slightly from the middle of the shield.

Cadets and Midshipmen

Cadets and midshipmen wear a gold Imperial Shield and Sword symbol on their service hats and dress hats.

Enlisted soldiers and sailors

Enlisted soldiers and sailors wear a 2-inches in diameter opaque silver circle with the silver Imperial Shield and Sword symbol in the center.

Non-Commissioned Officers

NCO's wear a 2-inches in diameter opaque gold circle with the silver Imperial Shield and Sword symbol in the center.

Sergeant Generals/Master Chief Petty Officer of the Imperial Navy

They wear a gold 2-inches in diameter opaque circle with silver Imperial Shield and Sword symbol in the center. A gold five-pointed star is in center of imperial shield, and the sword and shield are surrounded by silver crescents left and right of the sword.

Warrant Officers

Warrant officers wear 1-inch wide, 2 ½ inches long imperial shield and sword symbol that's all silver.

Company-Grade Commissioned Officers

These officers wear a 1-inch wide, 2 ½ inches long imperial shield and sword symbol, with shield being silver and the sword being gold.

Field-Grade Commissioned Officers

These officers wear a silver imperial warbird symbol with the warbird having 2 ½ inches wing span.

Flag-Grade Commissioned Officers

These officers wear a gold imperial warbird symbol with the warbird having 2 ½ inches wingspan.

Grand Admiral

The Grand Admiral wears a gold imperial warbird symbol with the warbird having 1 ½ inch wingspan with a silver five-pointed star pointing upwards raised in center of warbird's chest.

Commander-In-Chief of the Imperial Armed Forces

Same as the Grand Admiral, except the star in middle of imperial warbird has a hollowed out silver circle around the star with star's points being longer than circle's diameter. Also, a silver hollowed out circle starts in the small of imperial warbird's back all around behind each wing's center points all the way around.

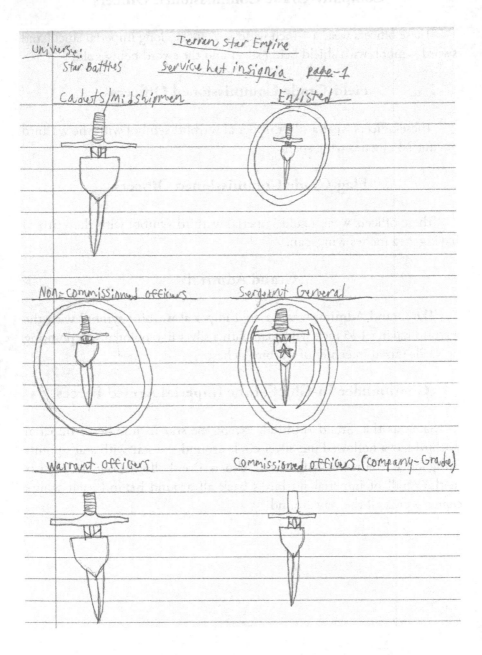

Universe:
Star Battles

Terran Star Empire
Service hat insignia   page-1

Cadets/Midshipmen   Enlisted

Non-commissioned officers   Sergeant General

Warrant officers   Commissioned officers (Company-Grade)

universe—
star Battles

Terran Star Empire
Service hat insignia   Page~2

commissioned officers (Field-Grade)

commissioned officers
(Flag-Grade)

Grand Admiral

Commander-IN-Chief of the
Imperial Armed Forces

SECTION FOUR:
Aide-de-Camp insignia

SECTION FOUR:
Aide-de-Camp Insignia

Aide-de-Camps are personal assistants or secretaries, to a person of high rank, usually a senior military officer or the Imperator/Imperatrix. They can also participate at ceremonial functions.

The badge of office is an auguilette, a braided cord that can come in different colors. Dress auguilettes are more elaborate, service auguilettes run under the arm and then over the shoulder, looping under the epaulettes. The number of loops depends on the person being aided.

Special insignia for aides are worn instead of MOS/Rating insignia, though the Aide retains his or her MOS/Rating colors on epaulettes, shoulder straps, stripes on pants, etc., etc. The Aide insignia has many variations, depending on the person being aided.

Aide to the
Imperator

Aide to the
Supreme chancellor

Aide to the
Grand Admiral

Aide to the
Supreme Admiral

Aide to the
chairman
Joint chiefs of Staff

Aide to a
chief of Staff

Aide to a
Fleet Admiral/
Marshal

Aide to an
Admiral/General

Aide to a
Vice-Admiral/
Lieutenant General

Aide to a
Rear Admiral/
Major General

Aide to a
Commodore/
Brigadier General

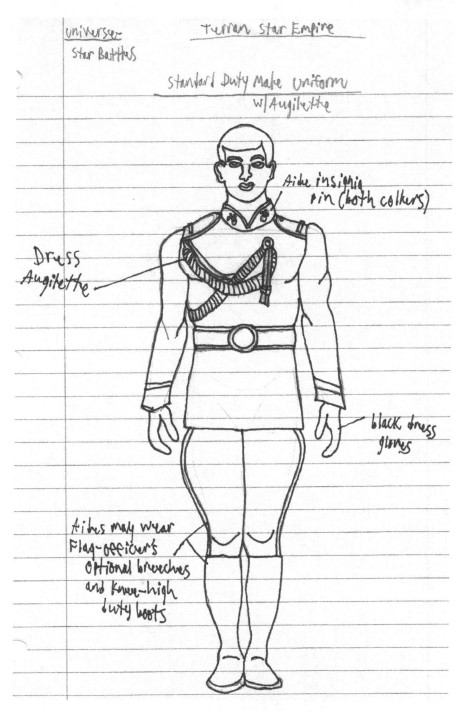

universe:
Star Battles

Turran Star Empire

Standard Duty Male Uniform
w/ Augilette

Aide insignia
pin (both colters)

Dress
Augilette

black dress
gloves

Aides may wear
Flag-officer's
Optional breeches
and knee-high
duty boots

SECTION FIVE:
Ship/Base Assignment Crests

These crests can come in a variety of shapes and colors. Some may even have inscriptions on them in modern Terran English or Latin languages. These crests will indicate the wearer's current starship, outpost, or base assignment is. They are located just above the right breast of the wearer on service, dress, and mess dress uniforms. Included are examples of two ship assignment crests of two of the ships of the Windstar class-Heavy Cruiser.

Task Force Commander's insignia . . .

This insignia consists of an armband and a yellow shoulder loop placed on epaulettes.

Task Force Commanders also wear a double-corded yellow cords with very thin black stripes on the cord. His/her direct assistant wears one cord.

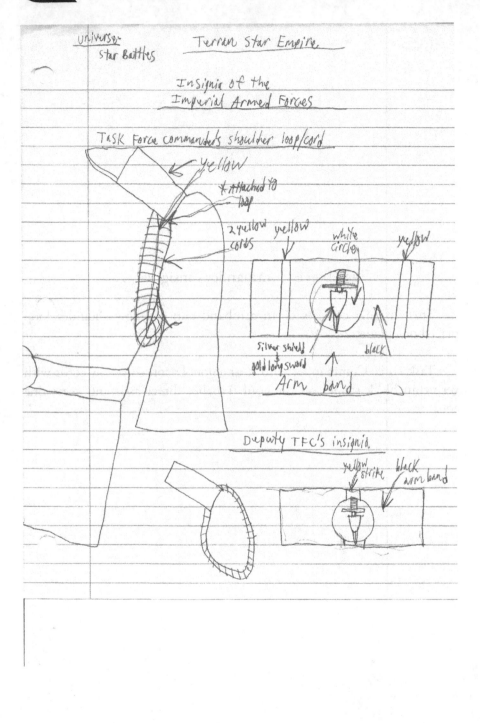

universe-
star Battles

Terran Star Empire

Insignia of the
Imperial Armed Forces

Task Force commander's shoulder loop/cord

yellow

* Attached to
loop

2 yellow
cords

yellow

white
circle

yellow

silver shield

gold long sword

black

Arm band

Deputy TFC's insignia

yellow
stripe

black
arm band

SECTION SIX:
Rank insignia pins

The Imperial Armed Forces have an elaborate rank system, with some ranks being added by the dystopic Jones Dynasty in the beginning of the Imperial Era. When the benevolent and honorable Jenkins Dynasty took power, they kept many of these new rank titles. Each rank has its own rank insignia pins. They are usually worn on epaulettes, shoulder boards, shoulder marks, shoulder straps, and some collars as indicated.

Cadets and midshipmen: are gold-colored ½ inch squares

Enlisted soldiers and sailors: are gold-colored ½ inch circles(pips)

Junior Non-Commissioned Officers: are gold-colored highly detailed ½ inch diamonds

Senior Non-Commissioned Officers: are silver-colored highly detailed ½ inch diamonds

Sergeant Generals/Senior Master Chief Petty Officer: are 1 ½ inch silver-colored diamond with silver crescents on left and right side of the diamond, with the crescents facing the diamond.

Warrant Officers: are silver-colored rectangles with black squares denoting grade

Company-grade Commissioned Officers: are gold-colored rectangles

Field-grade Commissioned Officers: are gold-colored 5-pointed stars

Flag-grade Commissioned Officers: are silver-colored 5-pointed stars

Marshals/Supreme Marshals/Fleet Admirals/Supreme Admiral: are gold and silver-colored, eight-ray star bursts with the bottom-most ray being elongated.

Grand Admiral: a 1 ½ inch silver-colored star with elaborate crescents surrounding the star.

Commander-In-Chief: is a silver-colored eagle with wings outstretched, grasping a silver scroll in its talons. Its head faces to the left. Above the scroll on the eagle's chest, is a long sword(gold hilt with white blade) pointing down behind a silver shield.

Rank Insignia

Rank insignia pins (page 1)

Cadets and Midshipmen

1. Cadet 4th class/midshipman 4th class

2. Cadet 3rd class/midshipman 3rd class

3. Cadet 2nd class/midshipman 2nd class

4. Cadet 1st class/midshipman 1st class

Enlisted soldiers and sailors

1. Private 3rd class/crewman 3rd class

2. Private 2nd class/crewman 2nd class

3. Private 1st class/crewman 1st class

4. Lance corporal/private major/crewman major

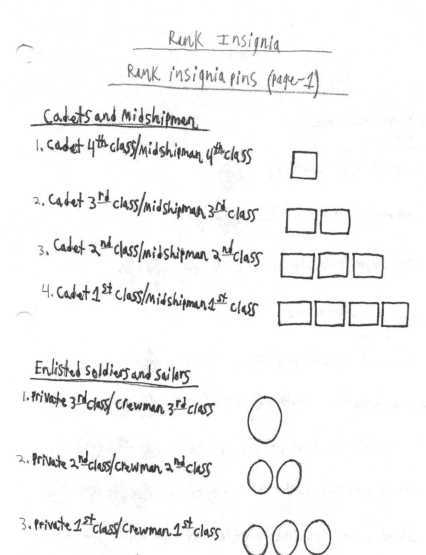

Rank Insignia

Rank insignia pins (page-2)

Junior Non-Commissioned Officers

1. Corporal/Petty officer 3rd class

2. Sergeant/Petty officer 2nd class

3. Staff Sergeant/Petty officer 1st class

Senior Non-commissioned Officers

1. Sergeant 1st class/chief Petty officer 3rd class

2. Master Sergeant/chief Petty officer 2nd class

3. Sergeant Major/chief Petty officer 1st class

4. Command Sergeant Major/Master chief Petty officer

5. Sergeant General/Senior Master chief Petty officer

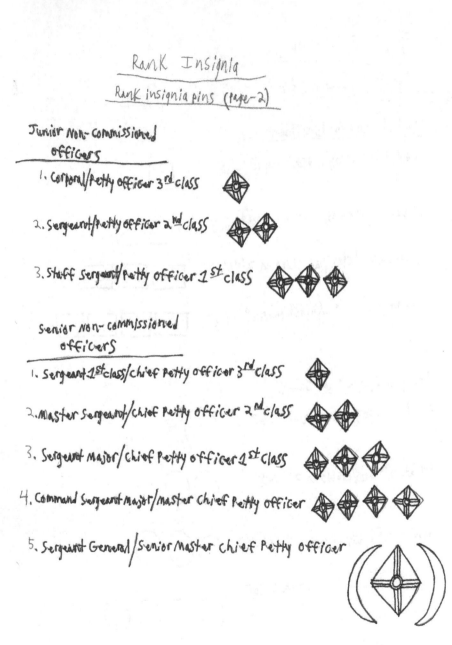

Rank Insignia

Rank insignia pins (page-3)

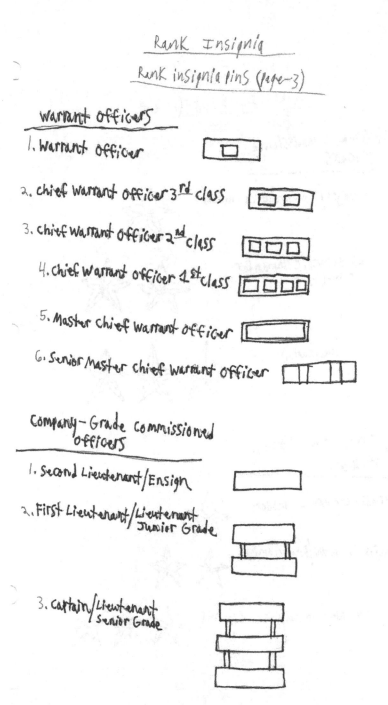

Warrant Officers

1. Warrant officer

2. chief warrant officer 3rd class

3. chief warrant officer 2nd class

4. chief warrant officer 1st class

5. Master chief warrant officer

6. Senior Master chief warrant officer

Company-Grade commissioned officers

1. Second Lieutenant/Ensign

2. First Lieutenant/Lieutenant Junior Grade

3. Captain/Lieutenant Senior Grade

Rank Insignia
Rank insignia pins (page-4)

Field-Grade Commissioned officers

1. Major/Lieutenant commander

2. Lieutenant/commander colonel

3. colonel/captain

Flag-Grade Commissioned officers

1. Brigadier General/commodore

2. Major General/Rear Admiral

3. Lieutenant General/vice-Admiral

General/Admiral

Marshal/Fleet Admiral

Supreme Marshal/
Vice-Supreme Admiral

Supreme Admiral

Grand Admiral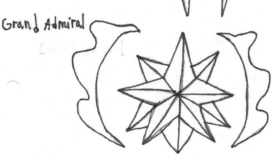

Commander-In-chief
of the
Imperial Armed Forces
(Imperator/Imperatrix)

SECTION SEVEN:
Rank insignia stripes

All ranks have rank insignia stripes, except for pay grade E-1.

Cadets and Midshipmen: have thin gold stripes on cuffs.

Enlisted and Non-Commissioned Officers, soldiers, and sailors: rank insignia stripes are yellow-colored chevrons, rockers, crescents, and stars placed upon both shoulders of indicated uniform types. Basic combat trainees who are squad guides get one thin black stripe on cuff of their training uniforms, platoon guides wear two thin black stripes on the cuffs of their training uniform.

Warrant Officers: Warrant Officers wear silver-colored regular and broad stripes, placed on their cuffs on uniforms as indicated.

Commissioned Officers: Commissioned Officers wear gold-colored regular and broad stripes, placed on cuffs of uniforms as indicated.

Rank Insignia
Rank insignia stripes (type-1)

Cadets and Midshipmen

1. cadet 4th class/midshipman 4th class

2. Cadet 3rd class/midshipman 3rd class

3. cadet 2nd class/midshipman 2nd class

4. Cadet 1st class/midshipman 1st class

Enlisted Soldiers and Sailors

1. private 3rd class/crewman 3rd class   (no insignia stripe)

2. private 2nd class/crewman 2nd class

3. private 1st class/crewman 1st class

Rank Insignia
Rank insignia stripes (page-2)

4. ~~Private Major~~/Crewman Major
Lance corporal/

Junior Non-Commissioned
officers

1. Corporal/Petty officer 3rd class

2. Sergeant/Petty officer 2nd class

3. Staff Sergeant/Petty officer 1st class

Rank Insignia

Rank insignia stripes (page-3)

<u>Senior Non-Commissioned Officers</u>

1. Sergeant 1st class/chief petty officer 3rd class

2. Master Sergeant/chief petty officer 2nd class

3. Sergeant Major/chief petty officer 1st class

Rank Insignia
Rank insignia stripes (page-4)

4. command sergeant Major/Master chief Petty officer

5. Sergeant General/Senior Master chief petty officer

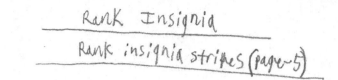

Rank Insignia

Rank insignia stripes (page~5)

warrant officers

1. warrant officer

chief
2. Warrant officer 3rd class

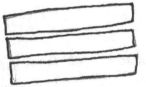

chief
3. Warrant officer 2nd class

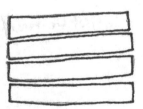

4. Chief warrant officer 1st class

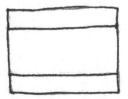

5. Master chief warrant officer

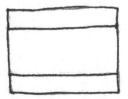

<u>Rank Insignia</u>

<u>Rank insignia stripes (page~6)</u>

6. Senior Master chief warrant officer

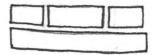

<u>Company-Grade commissioned officers</u>

1. Second Lieutenant/Ensign

2. First Lieutenant/Lieutenant Junior Grade

3. Captain/Lieutenant senior Grade

Rank Insignia
Rank insignia stripes (page-7)

Field-Grade commissioned officers

1. major/Lieutenant commander

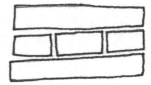

2. Lieutenant colonel/Commander

3. colonel/captain

Rank Insignia
Rank insignia stripes (page-8)

Flag- Grade commissioned officers

1. Brigidair General/commodore

2. Major General/Rear Admiral

3. Lieutenant General/Vice-Admiral

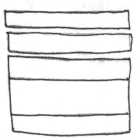

Rank Insignia

Rank insignia stripes (page-9)

4. General/Admiral

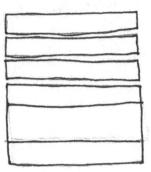

5. Marshal/Fleet Admiral

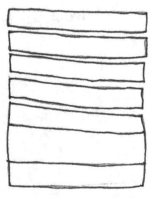

Rank Insignia

Rank insignia stripes (page-10)

6. Supreme Marshal/
Vice-Supreme Admiral

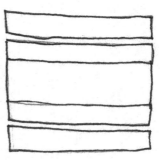

7. Supreme Admiral

Rank Insignia

Rank insignia stripes (page-11)

Grand Admiral

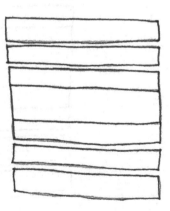

Commander- In- Chief of the
Imperial Armed Forces
(Imperator/Imperatrix)

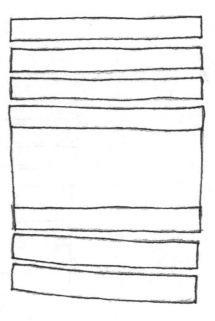

CHAPTER TWO:
Uniforms

Welcome to the second chapter of this manual. In this chapter is a huge selection of uniforms and their variances. Not all uniforms are shown, but a great many are shown nonetheless. Your uniforms should present a neat, clean appearance. Per orders from his majesty the Commander-In-Chief of the Imperial Armed Forces(Imperator), all uniforms that those of the male gender may also be worn by the female gender. These are known as unisex uniforms, though the uniform a female may wear, will be custom-tailored to fit most body types of most species, humanoid or not. Generally, females have many more varieties of uniforms to choose from. The uniform of the day will be ordered by local unit commanders.

Color of tunics: The colors of the wearer's tunic shows the wearer's branch of service. They are as follows . . .

Imperial Navy= white tunics

Marine Corps= gray tunics

Army= Green tunics

Special Operations Forces= purple tunics

Imperial Stormtrooper(special shock troops)Legion= black tunics

piping colors on uniforms: there are different-colored piping on uniforms, according to the wearer's rank. This piping is on most epaulettes, shoulder boards, shoulder marks, shoulder straps, and collars as follows . . .

Enlisted soldiers and sailors= no piping

Cadets and Midshipmen= white piping

Non-Commissioned Officers= black piping

Warrant Officers= silver piping

Company-Grade Commissioned Officers= gold piping

Field-Grade Commissioned Officers= gold piping on top of silver piping

Flag-Grade Commissioned Officers= gold piping on top of gold piping

SECTION ONE:
Service Uniforms

Service uniforms are the standard duty uniforms, worn for regular duty operations.

Standard duty service uniform(class-A): This is the standard duty uniform worn by all ranks and genders. It comes with duty tunic, pants, belt, and sometimes the standard duty service hats, as well as black dress gloves, and standard calf-length black duty boots. The tunic is branch-colored with epaulettes and stand-up collar. The standard duty black pants are high-waist with an elastic waist band. The standard duty black service belt is fitted at the wearer's point between rib cage and top of hip bone. The standard buckle is square-shaped for enlisted personnel, circular-shaped for officers. Most service buckles are brass, though honor guards may wear silver buckles.

MOS/Rating insignia pins are worn centered on each front-side of the stand-up collar. An MOS/Rating-colored shoulder cord is worn, looping under the right epaulette. The duty tunic length goes down to meet the end on the wearer's crotch. Duty pants are usually not tucked into duty boots, instead, their length is worn tapered at the wearer's ankle. Some officers may wear duty breaches, who's length goes three inches below the knee; in which case, black, knee-high duty boots may be worn. Females may elect to wear high-heeled versions of these duty boots. Black duty socks are worn under duty boots.

Instead of any of the variants of the service hats, any variant of garrison hats may be worn. The uniform tunic is zipped up from the back. White standard underwear is to be worn. A white, long-sleeved, high-collared undershirt is also to be worn and tucked into duty pants. A second variant undershirt may be worn. This is a crew-necked low collar that's short-sleeved and tucked into duty pants. Yet there's a third variant, a white tank-top t-shirt may be worn, tucked into duty pants. Females must wear standard duty bra with most service uniforms. Identification "dog tags" is to be worn as well. Standard-duty French kepi-style hats may be worn instead of service hats.

Variant-1: This variant is much like the regular standard variant, but is issued to females only. This variant replaces the standard duty pants with the standard-duty skirt. The length of this skirt goes to just above the wearer's knee. The skirt is black-colored. Officers have MOS/Rating-colored stripes on sides of pants, shorts and skirts, as described in the previous chapter. Black calf-length duty boots may be worn, or knee-high length duty boots are worn. Females may elect to wear high-heeled versions of duty boots. This is, of course an optional variant. Females may elect to wear nude-colored pantyhose.

Variant-2: This uniform variant is issued to females. This uniform has a stand-up collar with epaulettes(or replaced by MOS/Rating-colored shoulder straps). The tunic's length goes down and ends just under the female's breasts, along the line the rib cage makes and unzipped from the front. Either black, high-waist duty pants are worn, or the low-waist variant is worn. The low-waist variant showing the female's abdominal area. Yet another variant, is a standard-length black duty skirt is worn. Or, a low-waist black duty mini-skirt is worn. Another variant, comes with the sleeves being 3/4ths-length, and a third variant with the sleeves being short-sleeved, yet another variant having no sleeves. Long-sleeve variant will have rank stripes. In case the mini-skirt is worn, thigh-high black duty boots may be worn.

Standard Duty Service Uniform(Class-B): These uniforms are very similar to Class-A uniforms, except Class-B uniforms are made of a lighter-weighed fabric and the standard duty class-b tunic is usually tucked in. These uniforms may either have epaulettes, or shoulder straps. They also zip up the front instead of the back.

Female optional variants: Females may elect to wear class-b tunics with either 3/4th-length sleeves, or a short-sleeved variant(males may wear this variant with standard duty pants or duty black standard-length duty shorts), or may elect to wear a sleeve-less variant(has shoulder straps instead of epaulettes). Also, females may elect to wear the standard duty optional length skirt, or standard duty black shorts(3/4th length sleeved variant or sleeve-less variant).

Dress Uniforms: Are similar to service duty uniforms, but worn for more formal occasions, award ceremonies for example.

Standard Dress Uniform: This uniform has a stand-up collar like standard dress uniforms, with appropriate rank-colored piping with MOS/Rating insignia centered on front of each collar. This uniform unzips from the front from mid-point between each collar, then zips 2 inches to the right, then all the way down to the dress tunic's length. Dress tunic length goes all the way down and ends at the wearer's crotch. The tunic is branch-colored, and standard service belt or dress belts. It buckles between the wearer's rib cage and top of the hip bone.

The cuffs are MOS/Rating-colored, and goes up to a point on the outside portion of the sleeves. Special piping "chevrons" border the colored area, depending on wearer's rank. Rank insignia pins are placed centered in the colored area, as well placed on the epaulets. Officers and non-commissioned officers may replace epaulets with shoulder boards and place rank insignia pins onto said shoulder boards. A white, long-sleeved undershirt is to be worn under tunic, as is white underwear. This uniform is for both genders. For women, white duty bra and underwear are to be worn. This uniform is worn with either standard duty high-waist duty pants, or standard white high-waist dress pants. Standard duty calf-length or knee-length duty boots may be worn, as well as service hats and black dress gloves.

Female variants—Woman may replace service or dress pants with standard-length service skirt, or ankle-length black service duty skirt or a white variant. Also, rank-colored waist sash may be worn, or MOS/Rating-colored waist sash may be worn.

Mess Dress Uniform: This uniform are even more formal than the standard dress uniforms. A white, high-collared tunic is worn with appropriate rank piping on top of collar, with light-weighed epaulets with shoulder marks looped around epaulets, displaying appropriate rank insignia. This tunic also displays appropriate rank stripes. A dress vest may be worn over tunic with MOS/Rating-colored cummerbund bun, or rank-colored waist sash, or MOS/Rating-colored waist sash. A standard mess dress jacket is also worn, colored by the wearer's branch of service. This jacket's cuffs are the same pattern as standard dress sleeves with regular-weighed epaulets or shoulder boards. White high-waist dress pants are worn as is black calf-length or knee-length duty boots are worn. Medals may be displayed on this uniform. Appropriate white-colored undergarments must also be worn.

Female variants—Females may replace pants with skirts. If skirts are worn, nude-colored or brown-colored pantyhose may be worn.

Optional uniforms: There are several variants for men and women. Not all optional uniforms will be described.

Wrap-around uniforms—There is a wrap-around tunic and standard pants uniform. It comes with wrap-around tunic, standard duty belt, standard high-waist duty pants and calf-length duty boots. The tunic is branch-colored with MOS/Rating-colored epaulettes or shoulder straps. Standard black breeches may be worn if wearing knee-high boots. Rank stripes are worn on long-sleeve variant, while short-sleeve, and sleeve-less variants have shoulder straps instead. Black dress gloves may be worn with long-sleeve version. Females may replace duty pants with optional standard-length duty skirt. MOS/Rating-colored waist sash may be worn or rank-colored waist sash may be worn.

Bomber Jacket—A bomber jacket may be worn. This jacket is very popular with pilots. Black dress gloves may be worn.

Wrap-Around Jacket—This jacket may be worn with black dress gloves.

All weather coat—This coat has epaulettes, is black-colored, and is long-length. It goes down to just below the knee. A standard duty belt may be worn. Rank insignia pins are worn on the epaulettes.

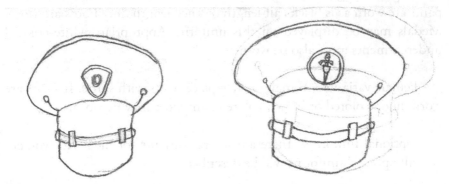

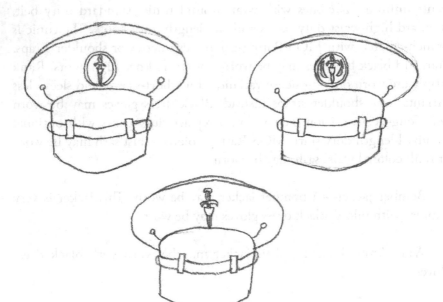

Imperial Armed Forces
buckles
page-1

Cadets/midshipmen
buckles:

Enlisted:

Non-commissioned
officers:

Sergeant
Generals:

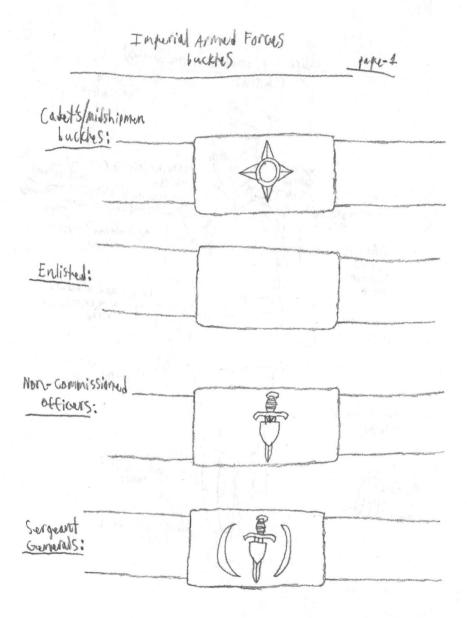

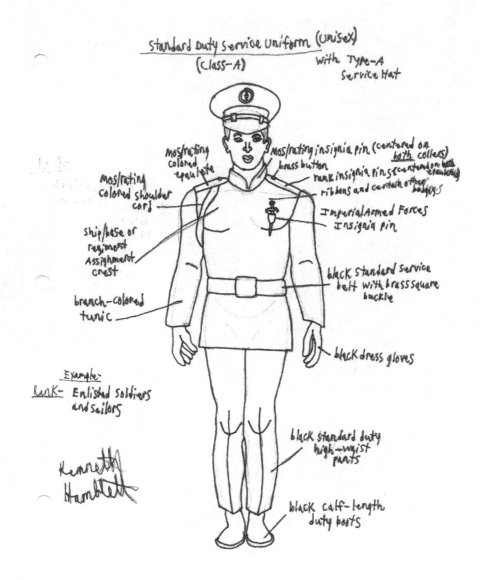

Standard Duty Service Uniform (unisex)
(Class-A)

with Type-A
Service Hat

mos/rating insignia pin (centered on both collars)

brass button

rank insignia pin (centered on both epaulets)

ribbons and certain other badges

Imperial Armed Forces
Insignia pin

mos/rating
colored
epaulete

mos/rating
colored shoulder
cord

ship/base or
regiment
Assignment
crest

branch-colored
tunic

black Standard Service
belt with brass square
buckle

black dress gloves

Example-
Rank- Enlisted Soldiers
and sailors

black standard duty
high-waist
pants

black calf-length
duty boots

Kenneth
Hamblett

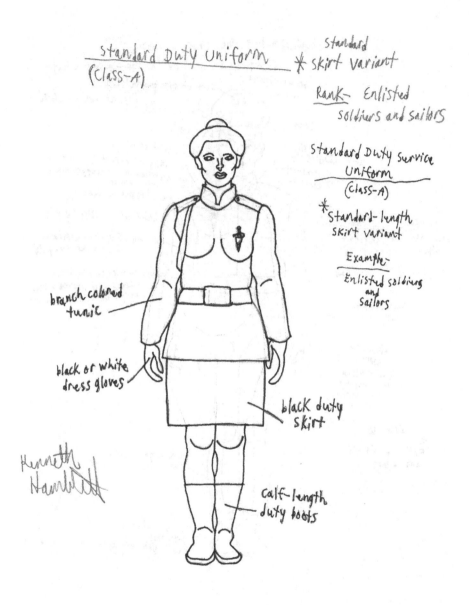

standard Duty Uniform
(Class-A)

standard
* skirt variant

Rank- Enlisted
soldiers and sailors

standard Duty service
Uniform
(Class-A)

* standard-length
skirt variant

Example-

Enlisted soldiers
and
sailors

branch colored
tunic

black or white
dress gloves

black duty
skirt

calf-length
duty boots

Kenneth
Hamblett

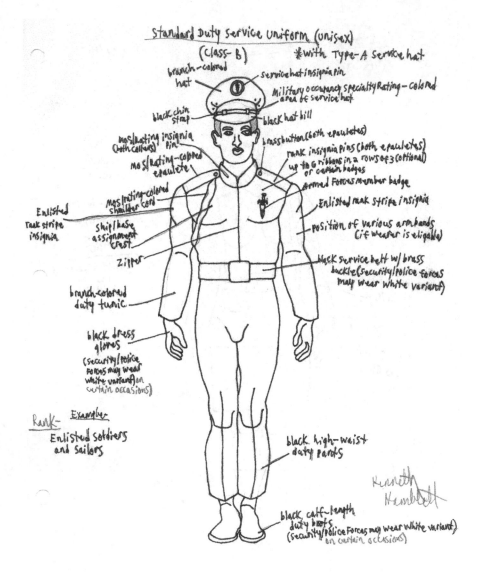

Standard Duty Service Uniform (unisex)
(Class-B)   ✳with Type-A service hat

branch-colored hat

service hat insignia pin

Military occupancy specialty Rating-colored area of service hat

black chin strap

black hat bill

mos/Rating insignia pin (both collars)

brass button (both epaulettes)

mos/Rating-colored epaulette

rank insignia pins (both epaulettes)

up to 6 ribbons in 2 rows of 3 (optional) or certain badges

armed Forces member badge

mos/Rating-colored shoulder cord

Enlisted rank stripe insignia

Enlisted rank stripe insignia

position of various armbands (if wearer is eligible)

ship/base assignment crest

zipper

black service belt w/ brass buckle (security/police forces may wear white variant)

branch-colored duty tunic

black dress gloves
(security/police forces may wear white variant on certain occasions)

black high-waist duty pants

Rank-
Examples-
Enlisted soldiers and sailors

black calf-length duty boots
(security/police forces may wear white variant) on certain occasions

Kenneth Hamblett

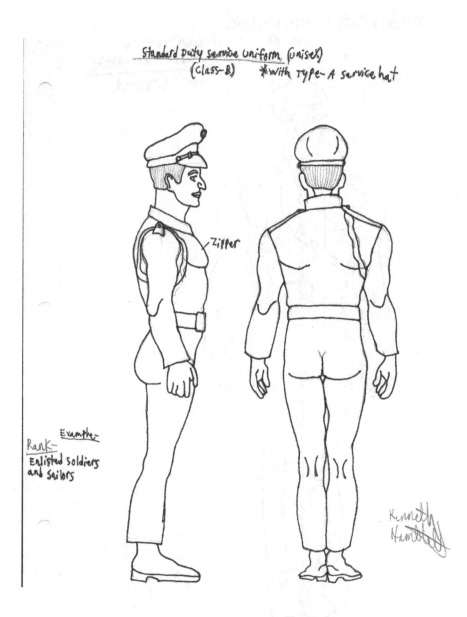

Standard Duty service Uniform (unisex)
(Class-B) *with Type-A service hat

Zipper

Example-
Rank-
Enlisted Soldiers
and Sailors

Kenneth
Humboldt

Standard Duty service uniform
(class-B)

w/ Security officer
tactical accessories
SO-TA type-1

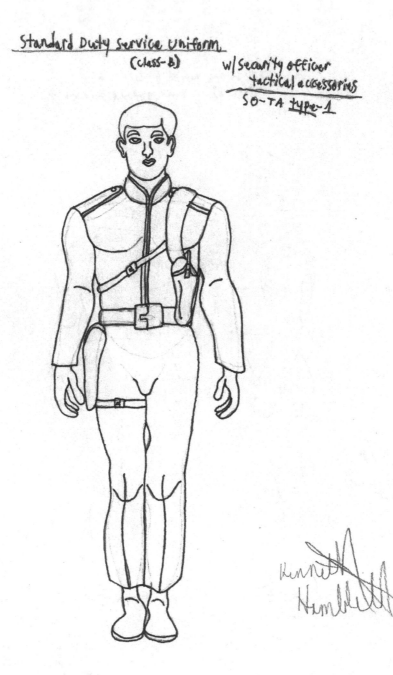

Standard Duty Service uniform
(class-B)

w/ security officer
tactical accessories
SO-TA type-2

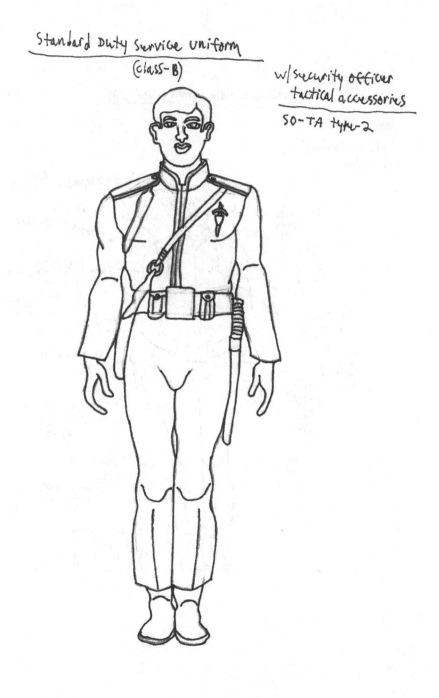

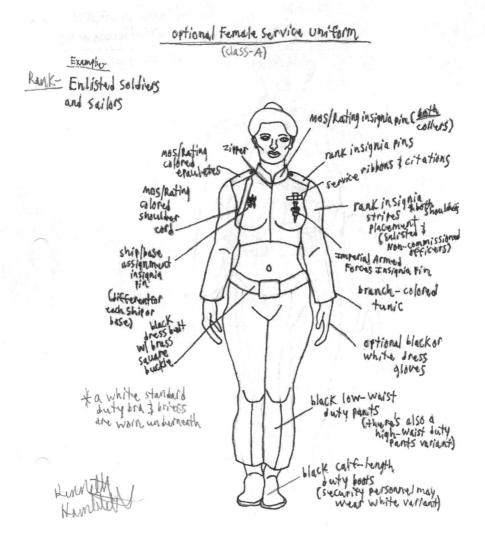

optional Female Service uniform
(class-A)

Example:

Rank- Enlisted soldiers
and sailors

mos/rating insignia pin (both collers)

mos/rating colored epaulettes

zipper

rank insignia pins

service ribbons & citations

mos/rating colored shoulder cord

rank insignia stripes *both shoulders placement & (Enlisted Non-commissioned officers)

Imperial Armed Forces Insignia pin

ship/base assignment insignia pin

(different for each ship or base)

branch-colored tunic

black dress belt w/ brass square buckle

optional black or white dress gloves

*a white standard duty bra & briefs are worn underneath

black low-waist duty pants

(there's also a high-waist duty pants variant)

black calf-length duty boots

(security personnel may wear white variant)

Kenneth Hamblett

Standard Duty Service Uniform
(Class-A)

Example
Rank- Captain
Branch- Imperial Navy
MOS- command corps
Race- caucasian
Terran

* Field-Grade
commissioned
officers

w/ ~~ship base~~ base
commander's
Badge

Standard Duty Service Uniform
(Class-A)

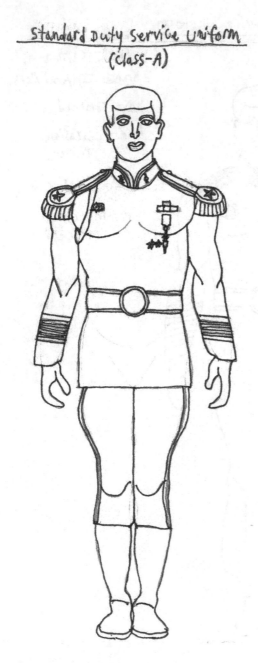

Example
Rank — commodore
Branch — Imperial Navy
MOS — Tactical corps
Race — Caucasian
       Terran

✳ Flag-Grade
commissioned officers

Optional Flag-Grade Commissioned officer's
Long Tunic

crew-collared short-sleeve undershirt (unisex)
w/ standard duty pants

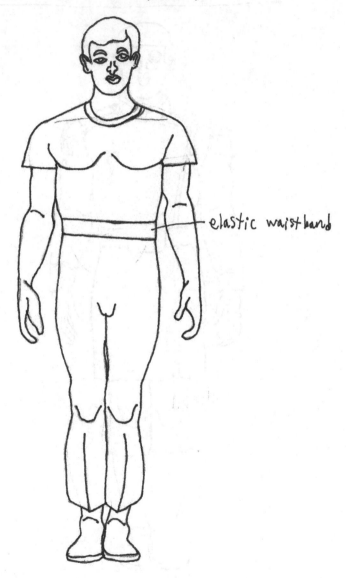

elastic waistband

Tank-top undershirt w/ (unisex) standard duty pants

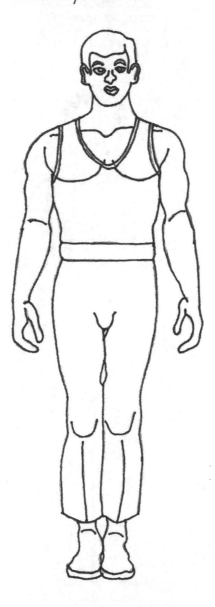

universe-
    Star Battles

Terran Star Empire

Female standard underwear
(standard bra and briefs)
          Variant
⨍ w/crew socks

Rank- All

Branch- All

MOS- All

SECTION TWO:
Dress Uniforms

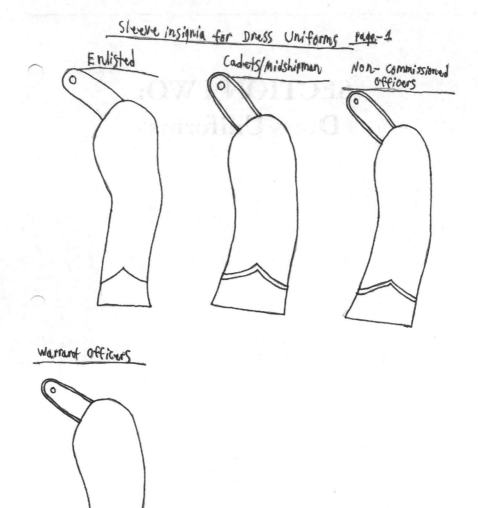

Sleeve insignia for Dress Uniforms   page-1

Enlisted   Cadets/Midshipman   Non- commissioned officers

Warrant Officers

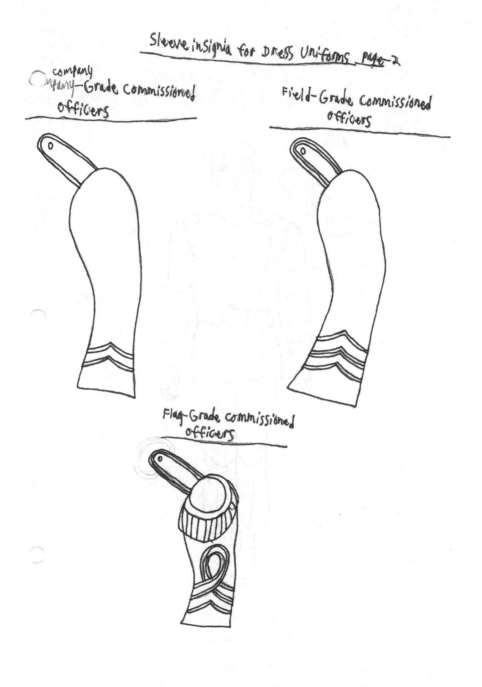

Sleeve insignia for Dress Uniforms, page 2

company
Company-Grade Commissioned
Officers

Field-Grade Commissioned
officers

Flag-Grade commissioned
officers

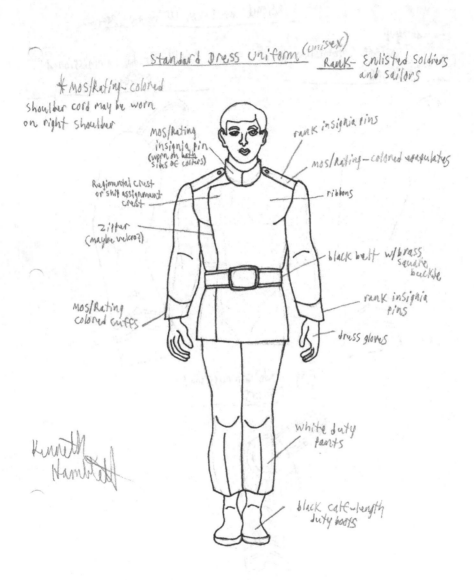

Standard Dress Uniform (unisex)   Rank- Enlisted Soldiers and sailors

*Mos/Rating-colored shoulder cord may be worn on right shoulder

Mos/Rating insignia pin (worn on both sides of collars)

rank insignia pins

mos/Rating-colored epaulates

Regimental crest or ship assignment crest

ribbons

zipper (maybe velcro?)

black belt w/brass square buckle

mos/Rating colored cuffs

rank insignia pins

dress gloves

white duty pants

black calf-length duty boots

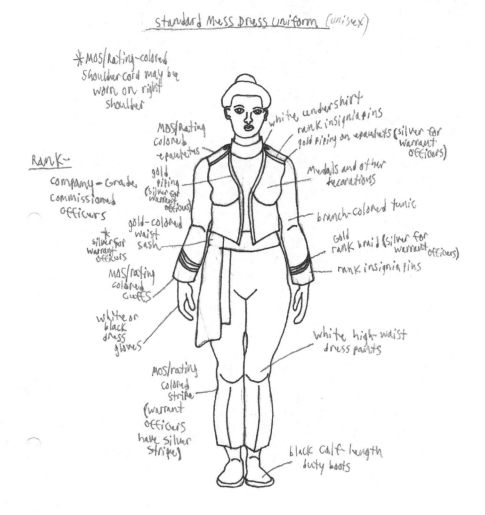

standard Mess Dress uniform (unisex)

* MOS/rating-colored
shoulder cord may be
worn on right
shoulder

MOS/rating
colored
epaulettes

white undershirt

rank insignia pins

gold piping on epaulettes (silver for
warrant
officers)

Rank~

company-grade
commissioned
officers

gold
piping
(silver for
warrant
officers)

Medals and other
decorations

branch-colored tunic

gold-colored
waist
sash

* silver for
warrant
officers

gold
rank braid (silver for
warrant officers)

rank insignia pins

MOS/rating
colored
cuffs

white or
black
dress
gloves

white high-waist
dress pants

MOS/rating
colored
stripe
(warrant
officers
have silver
stripes)

black calf-length
duty boots

SECTION THREE:
Medical Personnel Uniforms

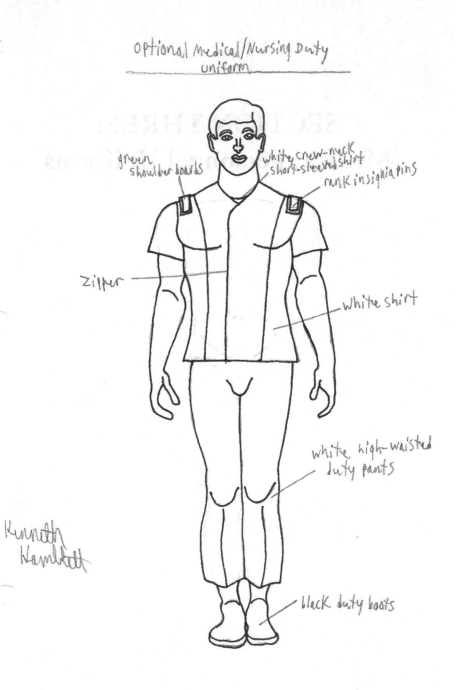

Optional Medical/Nursing Duty uniform

green shoulder boards

white, crew-neck short-sleeved shirt

rank insignia pins

zipper

white shirt

white, high-waisted duty pants

black duty boots

Kenneth Hamblett

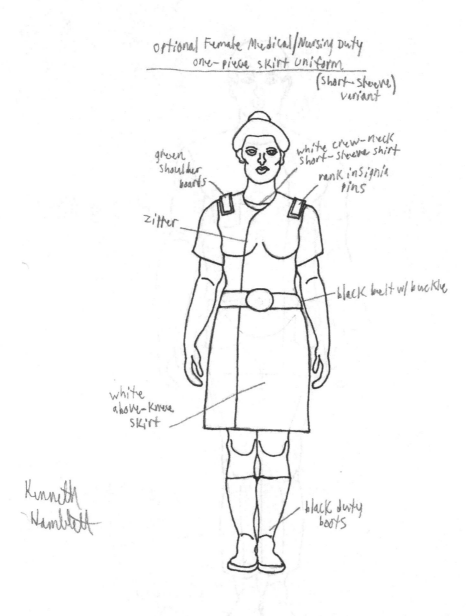

optional Female Medical/Nursing Duty
one-piece skirt uniform
(short-sleeve)
variant

green
shoulder
boards

white crew-neck
short-sleeve shirt

rank insignia
pins

zipper

black belt w/ buckle

white
above-knee
skirt

black duty
boots

Kenneth
Hamblett

standard physician's Lab coat
(may be worn w/a)
variety of
uniforms

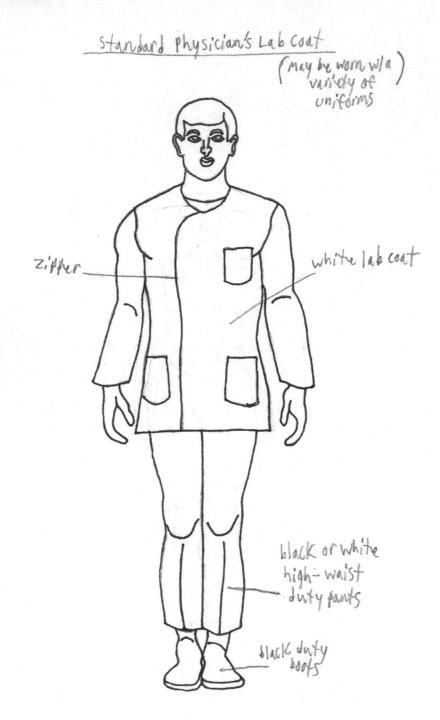

zipper

white lab coat

black or white
high-waist
duty pants

black duty
boots

Male Medical Technician's scrubs uniform

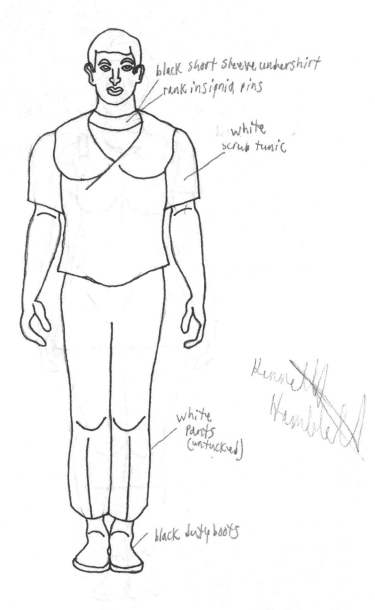

black short sleeve undershirt
rank insignia pins

white
scrub tunic

white
pants
(untucked)

black duty boots

optional Female one-piece mini-skirt
medical Duty uniform

(medical corpman)
short-sleeve
variant

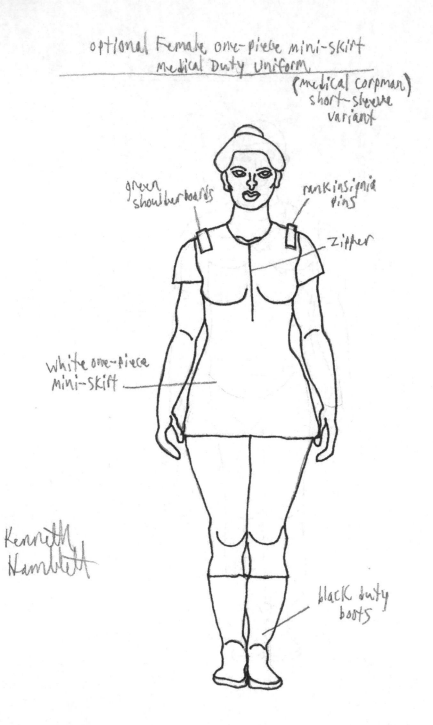

green
shoulderboards

rankinsignia
pins

zipper

white one-piece
mini-skirt

black duty
boots

Kenneth
Hamblett

Medical Technician's Jumpsuit

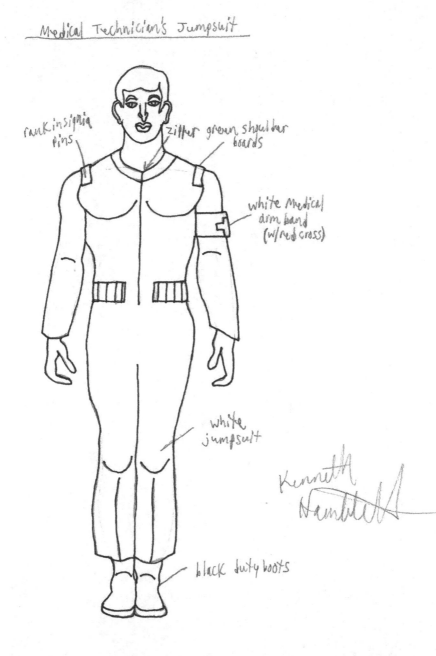

rank insignia pins

zipper green shoulder boards

white Medical arm band (w/ red cross)

white jumpsuit

Kenneth Hamtblett

black duty boots

SECTION FOUR:
Optional Uniforms

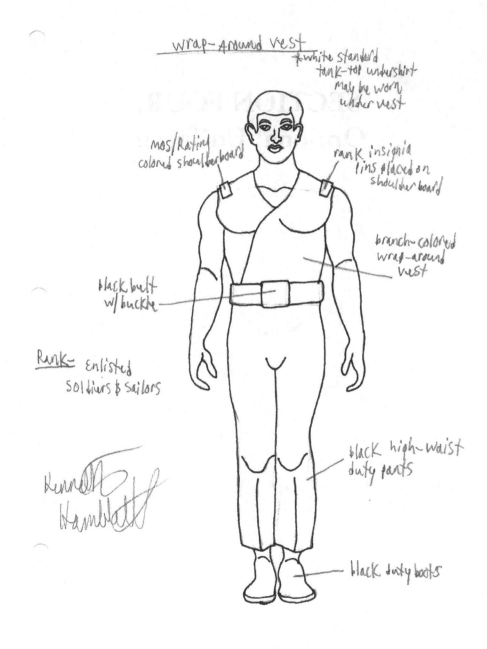

wrap-around vest
→ white standard
tank-top undershirt
may be worn
under vest

mos/Rating
colored shoulderboard

rank insignia
lins placed on
shoulderboard

branch-colored
wrap-around
vest

black belt
w/ buckle

Rank- Enlisted
Soldiers & Sailors

black high-waist
duty pants

black duty boots

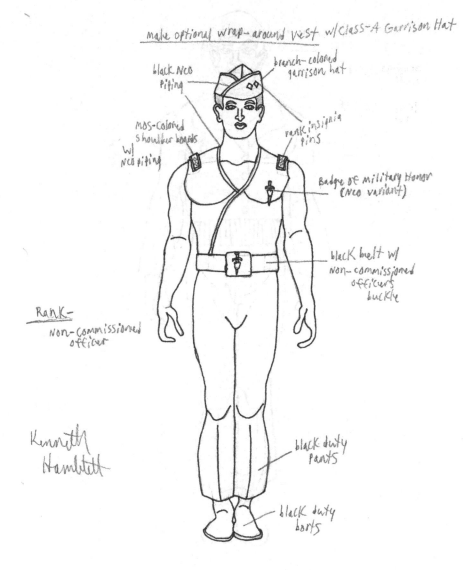

male optional wrap-around vest w/ class-A Garrison Hat

black NCO piting

branch-colored garrison hat

MOS-colored shoulder boards w/ NCO piping

rank insignia pins

Badge of military Honor (NCO variant)

black belt w/ Non-commissioned officers buckle

Rank-
Non-commissioned officer

black duty pants

black duty boots

Kenneth Hamblett

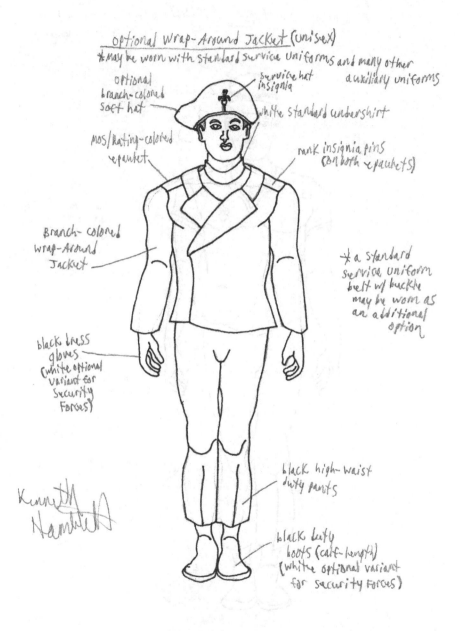

optional Wrap-Around Jacket (unisex)
*may be worn with standard service uniforms and many other auxiliary uniforms

optional branch-colored soft hat

service hat insignia

white standard undershirt

MOS/Rating-colored epaulet

rank insignia pins (on both epaulets)

Branch-colored Wrap-Around Jacket

*a standard service uniform belt w/ buckle may be worn as an additional option

black dress gloves (white optional variant for security forces)

black high-waist duty pants

black duty boots (calf-length) (white optional variant for security forces)

Optional Uniform (unisex) * Garrison-type hats may also be worn

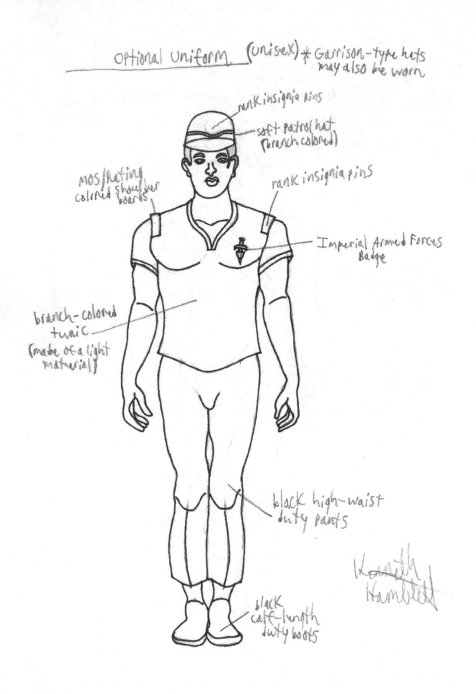

rank insignia pins

soft patrol hat (branch colored)

rank insignia pins

MOS/Rating colored shoulder boards

Imperial Armed Forces Badge

branch-colored tunic (made of a light material)

black high-waist duty pants

black calf-length duty boots

Optional Uniform

* MOS/Rating shoulder cord may be worn

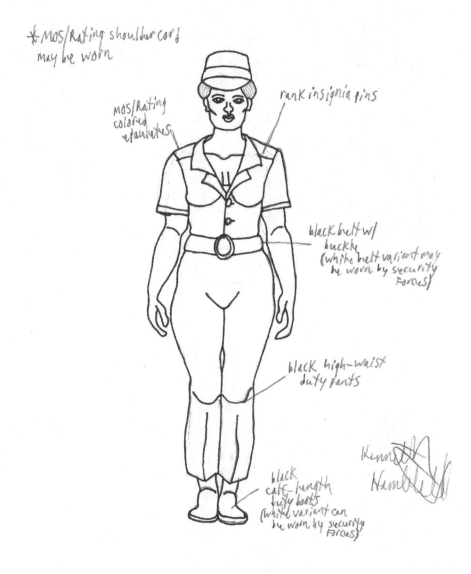

MOS/Rating colored epaulettes

rank insignia pins

black belt w/ buckle (white belt variant may be worn by security forces)

black high-waist duty pants

black calf-length duty boots (white variant can be worn by security forces)

optional Wrap-Around Uniform
variant-?

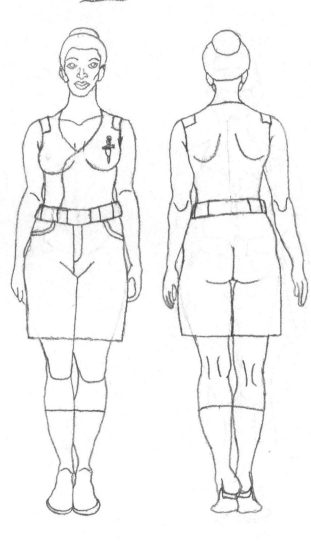

universe-
Star Battles

Terran Star Empire

Female T-130 Optional
uniform

* w/ Badge of the New Order

Rank- crewman 2nd
class

Branch- Imperial Navy

MOS- Medical corps

Race- Caucasian
Terran

Universe-
    Star Battles

Terran Star Empire

Female T-130 optional
        uniform

Rank- Crewman 2nd class
Branch- Imperial Navy
MOS- Medical Corps
Race- Caucasian Terran

Universe-
Star Battles

Terran Star Empire

Female T-130 optional
uniform

Rank- Crewman 2nd
class

Branch- Imperial Navy

MOS- Medical corps

Race- Caucasian
Terran

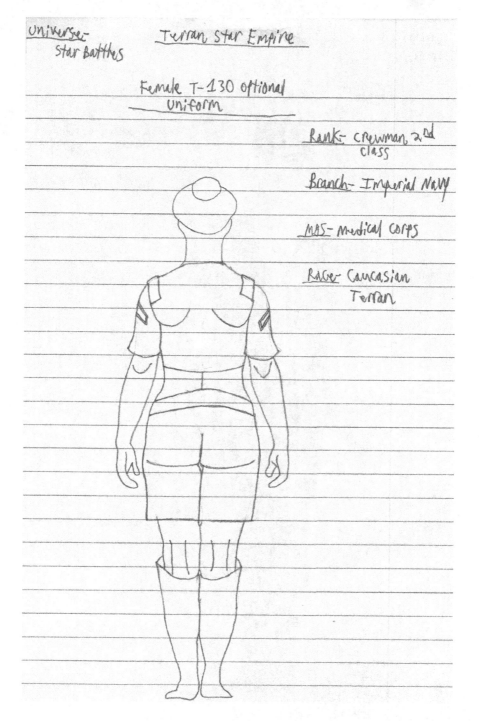

Universe-
Star Battles

Terran Star Empire

optional Male vest w/ standard undershirt

Rank- Sergeant
General

Branch- Marine corps

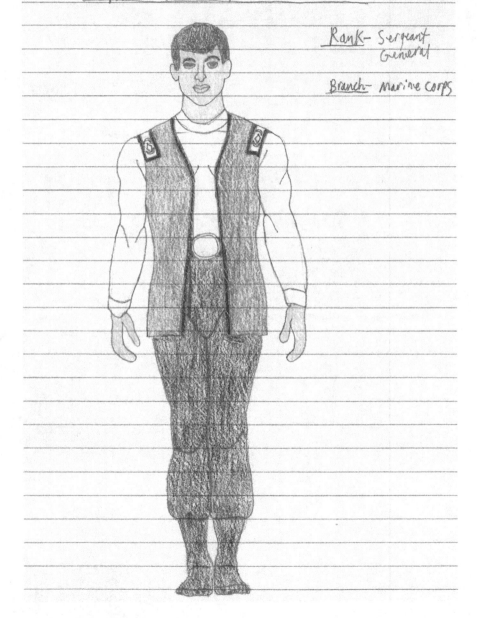

Universe-
Star Battles

Terran Star Empire

Optional Female Uniform

Rank- captain

Branch- Army

SECTION FIVE:
Utility and combat uniforms

Radiation suit (unisex)

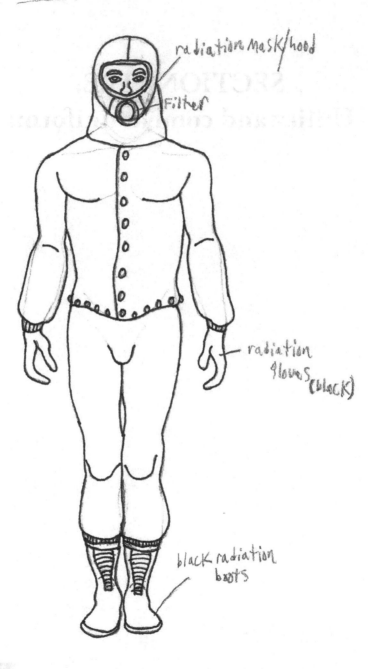

radiation mask/hood

Filter

radiation gloves (black)

black radiation boots

standard Thermal Undergarments (unisex)

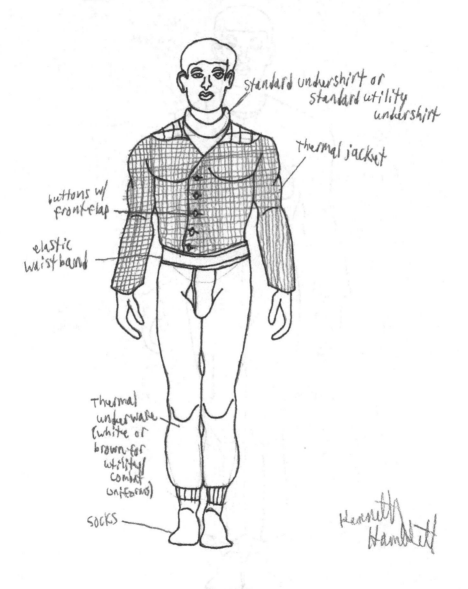

standard undershirt or
standard utility
undershirt

thermal jacket

buttons w/
front flap

elastic
waistband

Thermal
underwear
(white or
brown for
utility/
combat
uniforms)

socks

Kenneth
Hamblett

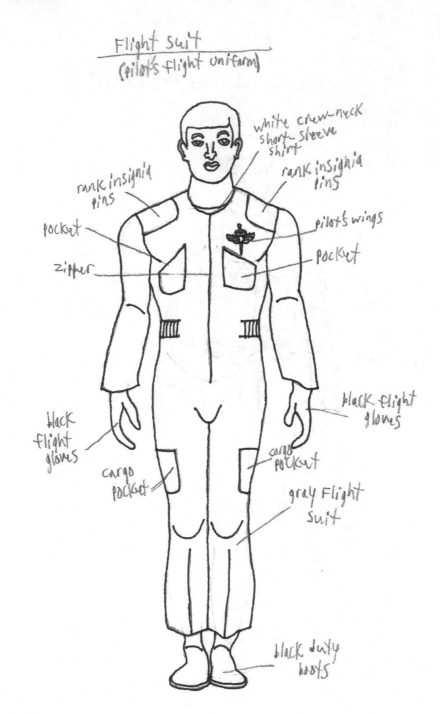

Flight suit
(pilot's flight uniform)

white crew-neck short-sleeve shirt

rank insignia pins

rank insignia pins

pilot's wings

pocket

pocket

zipper

black flight gloves

black flight gloves

cargo pocket

cargo pocket

gray flight suit

black duty boots

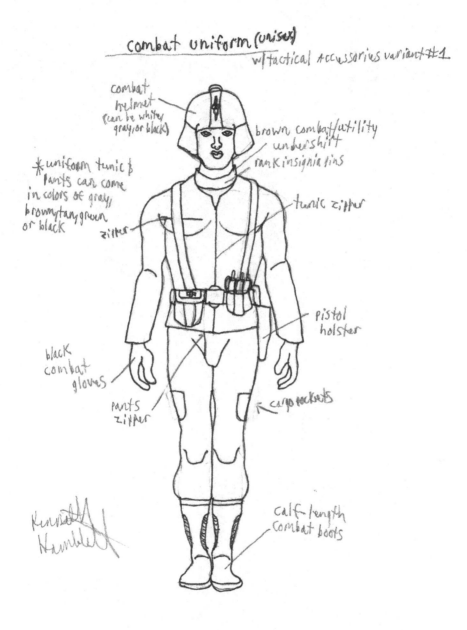

combat uniform (unisex)
w/ tactical Accessories variant #1

combat helmet (can be white, gray, or black)

brown combat/utility undershirt

rank insignia tins

*uniform tunic & pants can come in colors of gray, brown, tan, green or black

tunic zipper

zipper

pistol holster

black combat gloves

pants zipper

cargo pockets

calf-length combat boots

SECTION SIX:
Miscellaneous Uniforms
(Some quick sketched, some not)

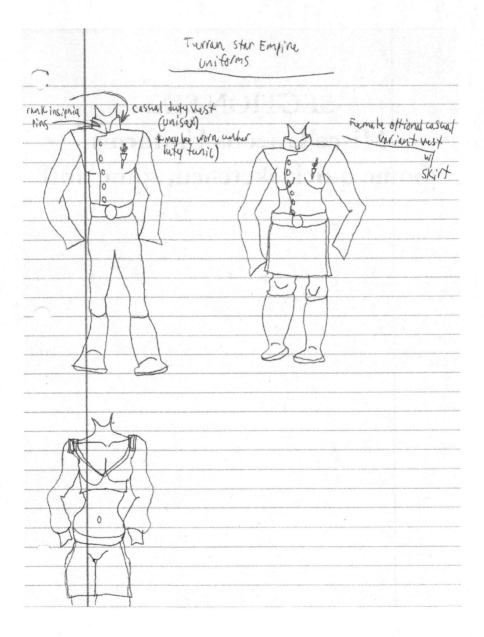

Terran star Empire
uniforms

rank insignia pins

casual duty vest
(unisex)

*may be worn under
duty tunic)

Female optional casual
variant vest
w/
skirt

elastic band

rank stripes

Kenneth Hamblett

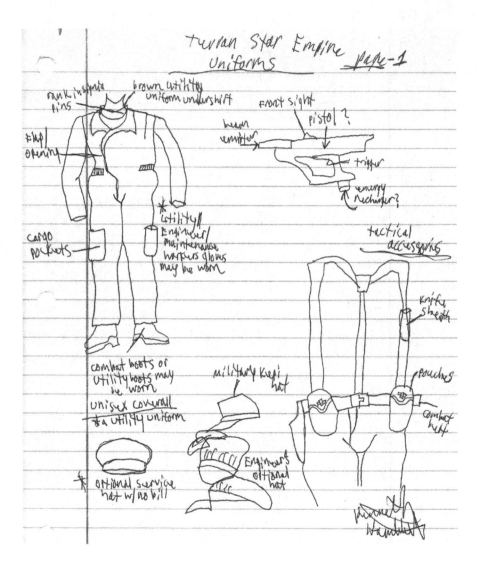

uniform designs

energy carbine/pistol

beam emitter

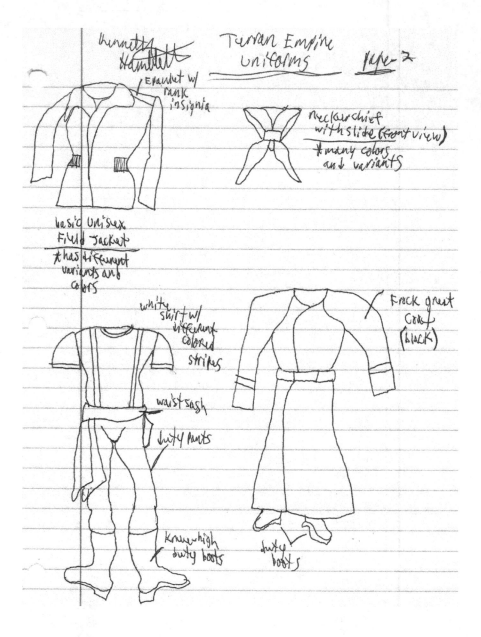

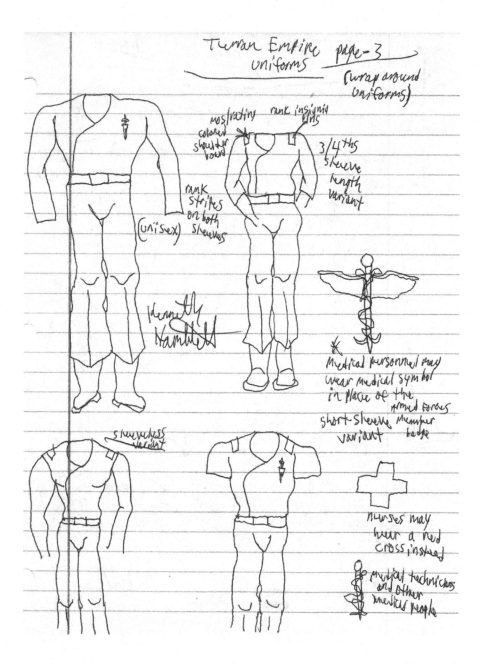

Turran Empire page-3
uniforms
(wrap around
uniforms)

non/rating
colored
shoulder
board

rank insignia
pins

3/4ths
sleeve
length
variant

rank
stripes
on both
sleeves

(unisex)

Kenneth
Hamblett

Medical personnel may
wear medical symbol
in place of the
armed forces
short-sleeve member
variant badge

sleeveless
variant

nurses may
wear a red
cross, instead

medical technicians
and other
medical people

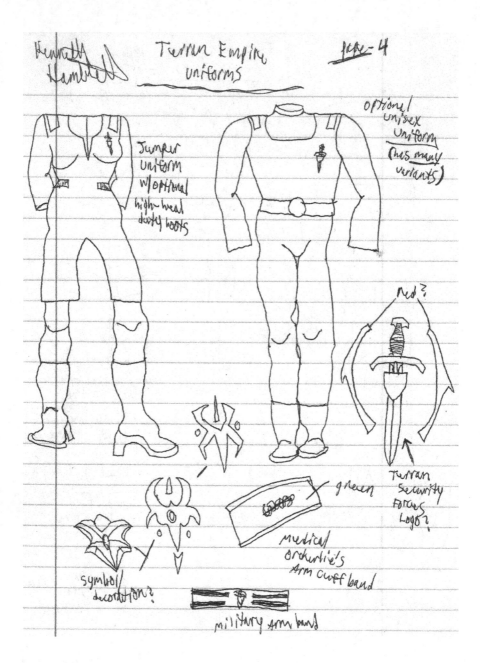

Kenneth Hamblett

Terran Empire
uniforms

page - 4

optional
unisex
uniform
(has many
variants)

Jumper
uniform
w/optional
high-heal
dusty boots

Red?

Terran
security
forces
Logo?

green

medical
orchurtie's
Arm cuff band

symbol
decoration?

military arm band

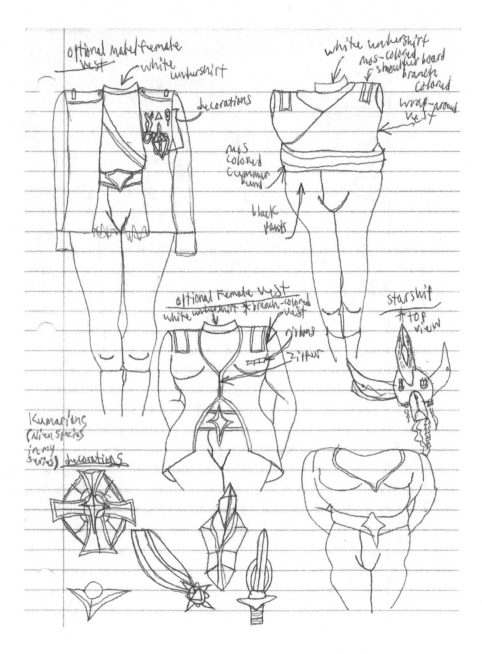

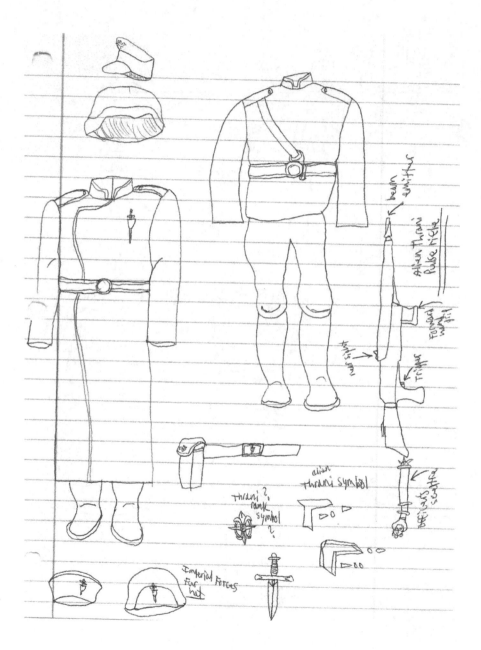

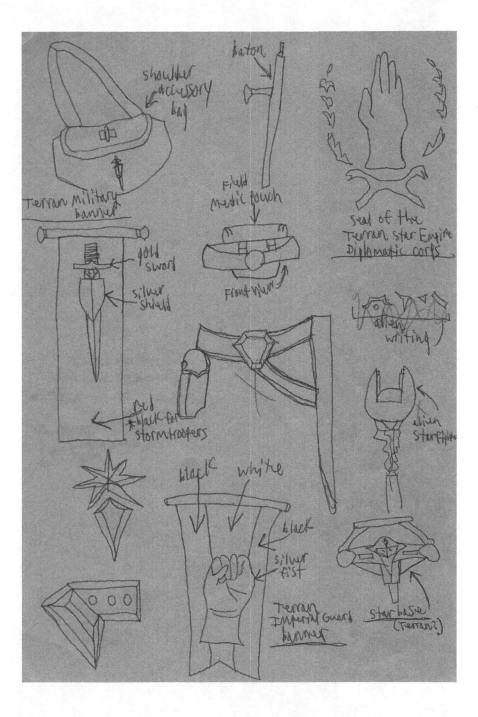

Different military
Hats   page - 1

Front   Side

Storm Trooper
combat helmet

optional desert
duty patrol hat

Storm Troopers
optional patrol
hat

storm troopers
optional kepi hat

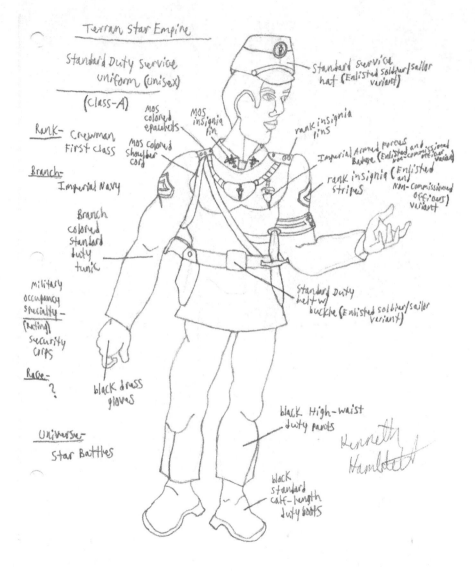

Terran Star Empire

Standard Duty service
uniform (Unisex)

(Class-A)

Rank- Crewman
First class

Branch-
Imperial Navy

Branch
colored
standard
duty
tunic

military
occupancy
specialty-
(Rating)
security
corps

Race-
?

Universe-
Star Battles

MOS
colored
epaulets

MOS
insignia
pin

MOS colored
shoulder
cord

black dress
gloves

standard service
hat (Enlisted soldier/sailor
variant)

rank insignia
pins

Imperial Armed Forces and
Badge (Enlisted and
non-commissioned officer variant)

rank insignia (Enlisted
and
Non-Commissioned
Officers)
variant

rank insignia
stripes

Standard Duty
belt w/
buckle (Enlisted soldier/sailor
variant)

black High-waist
duty pants

black
standard
calf-length
duty boots

Kenneth
Hamblett

univurser
star Battles

Terran Star Empire.

Army police officer

Standard Duty service
uniform
(Class-A)

Rank- Lieutenant SR Grade/
Captain

MOS- Tactical corps

w/ Type-B
service hat

Kenneth
Hamblett

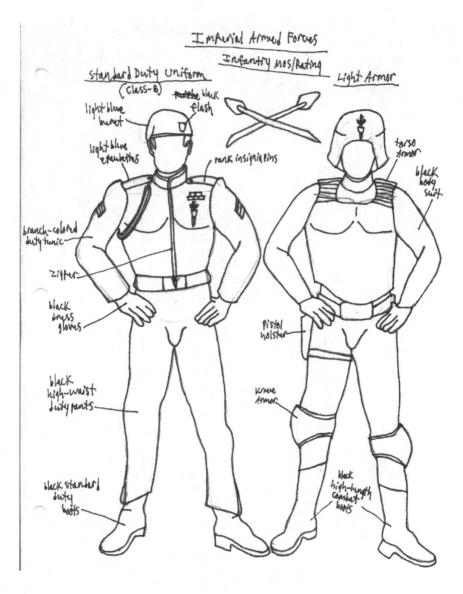

Imperial Armed Forces

Infantry mos/Rating

Standard Duty Uniform (Class-B)

Light Armor

black flash

light blue beret

light blue epaulettes

rank insignia pins

branch-colored duty tunic

zipper

black dress gloves

black high-waist duty pants

black standard duty boots

torso armor

black body suit

pistol holster

knee armor

black high-length combat boots

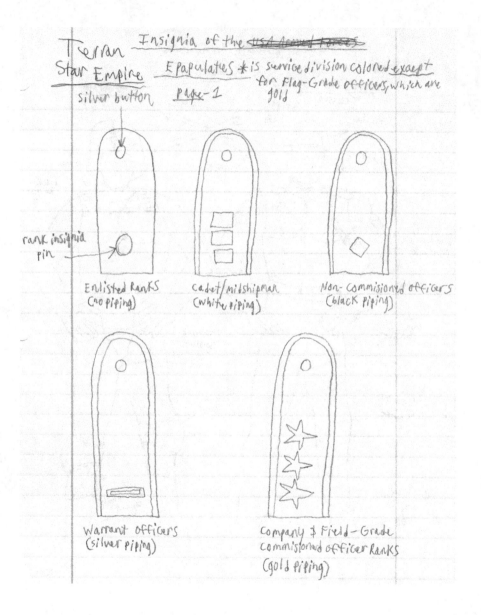

Terran Star Empire

Insignia of the ~~USA Armed Forces~~

Epapulates * is service division colored except for Flag-Grade officers, which are gold

silver button

Page-1

rank insignia pin

Enlisted Ranks (no piping)

Cadet/midshipman (white piping)

Non-Commisioned officers (black piping)

Warrant officers (silver piping)

Company & Field-Grade commissioned officer ranks (gold piping)

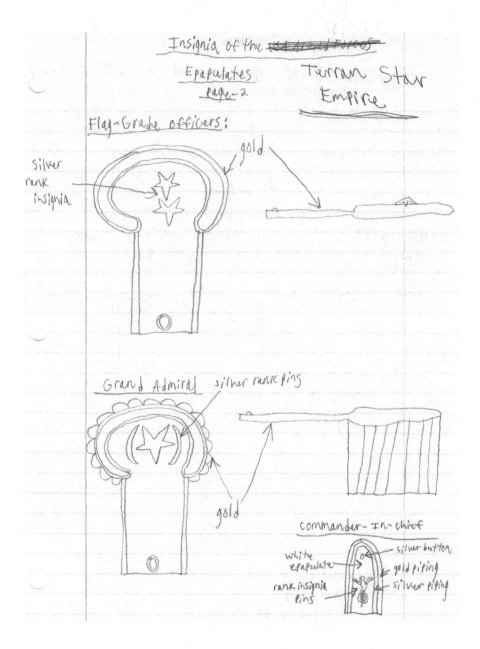

Insignia of the ~~US Armed Forces~~

Epapulates
page-2

Terran Star
Empire

Flag-Grade officers:

silver
rank
insignia

gold

Grand Admiral   silver rank pins

gold

commander-in-chief

white
epapulate

rank insignia
pins

silver button
gold piping
silver piping

Insignia

Shoulder Boards ✳ is service division colored

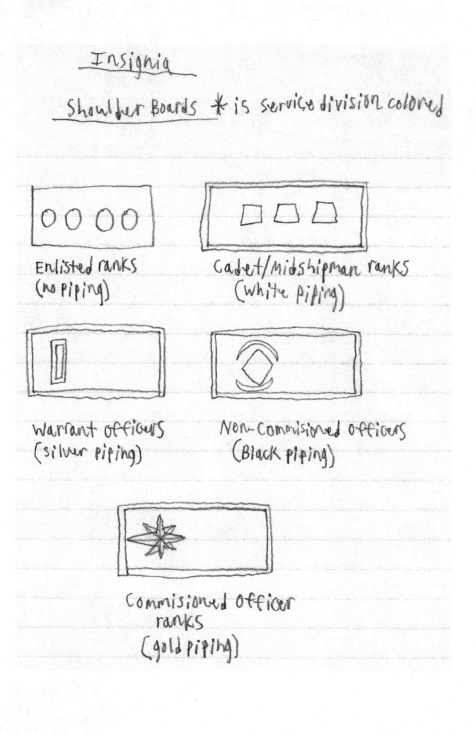

Enlisted ranks
(no piping)

Cadet/Midshipman ranks
(white piping)

Warrant officers
(silver piping)

Non-Commisioned officers
(Black piping)

Commisioned officer
ranks
(gold piping)

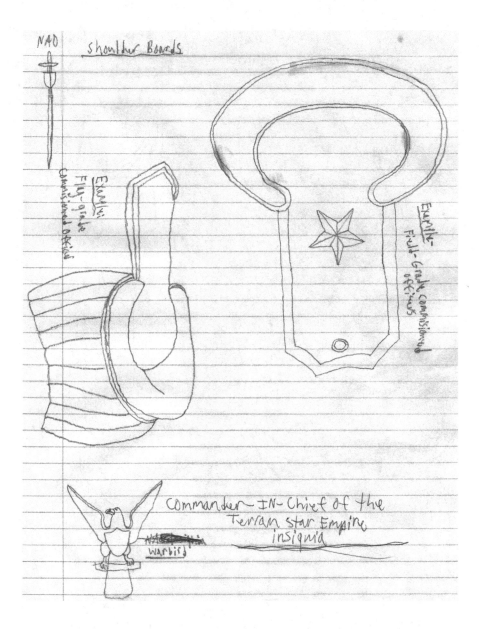

NAO

shoulder Boards

Example: Flag-grade commissioned officers

Example- Field-Grade commissioned officers

Commander-In-Chief of the Terran Star Empire insignia

Warbird

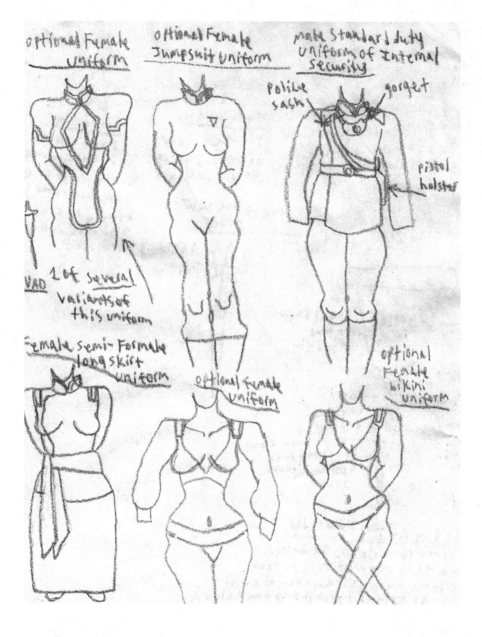

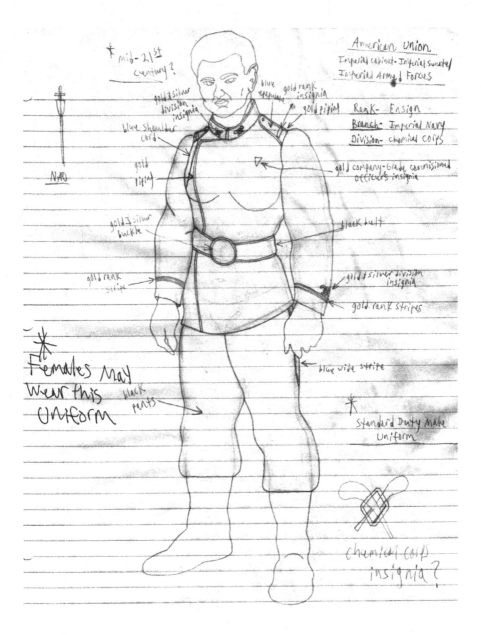

* Mid-21st century?

American Union
Imperial cabinet - Imperial senate/
Imperial Army & Forces

gold & silver division insignia
blue epaulena
gold rank insignia
gold piping
blue shoulder cord
gold piping
gold & silver buckle

Rank - Ensign
Branch - Imperial Navy
Division - chemical corps

gold company-Grade commissioned officer's insignia

black belt

gold rank stripe
gold & silver division insignia
gold rank stripes

NAD

Females May Wear this Uniform
black pents
blue wide stripe

* Standard Duty Male Uniform

chemical corps insignia?

Imperial Army Forces

Male Hell hat

color of hat differentiates between men with great armed services

* Any Uniform that men wear women may wear it as well. women just have many more uniform variants to choose from.

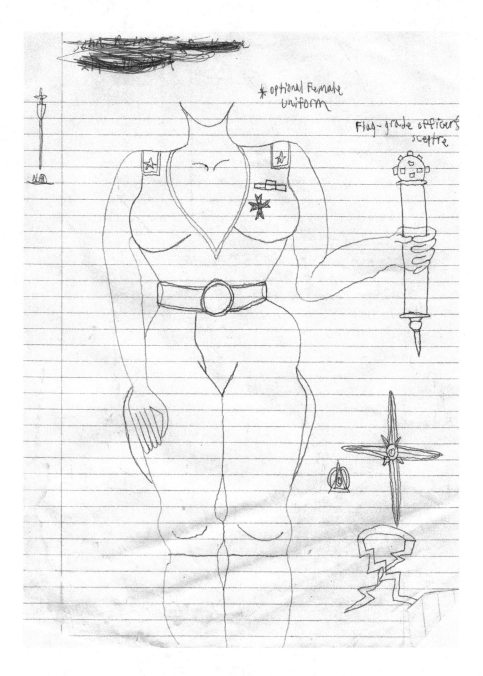

* optional Female
uniform

Flag-grade officers
sceptre

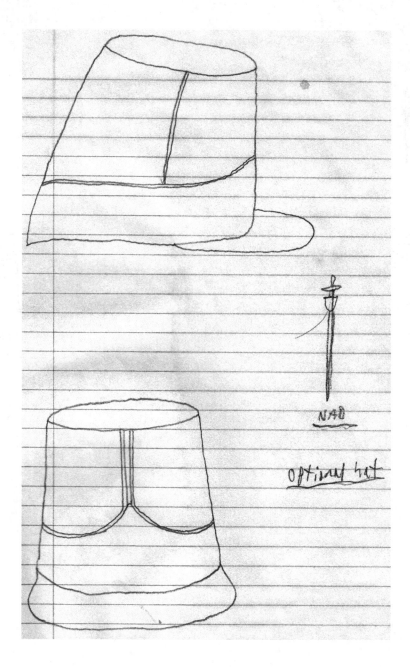

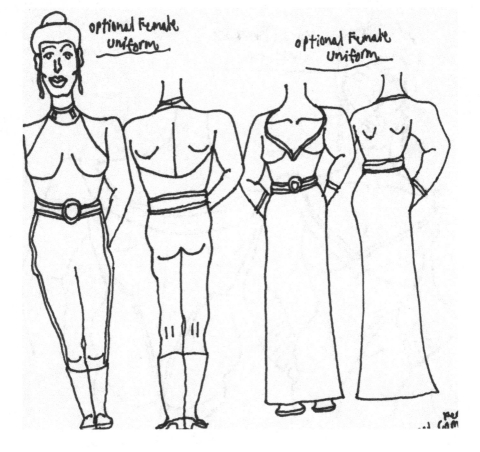

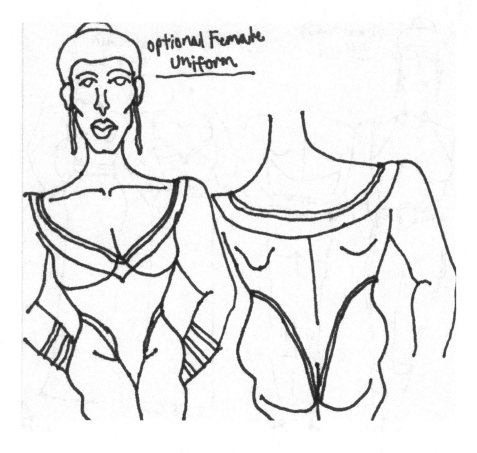

optional Female
Uniform

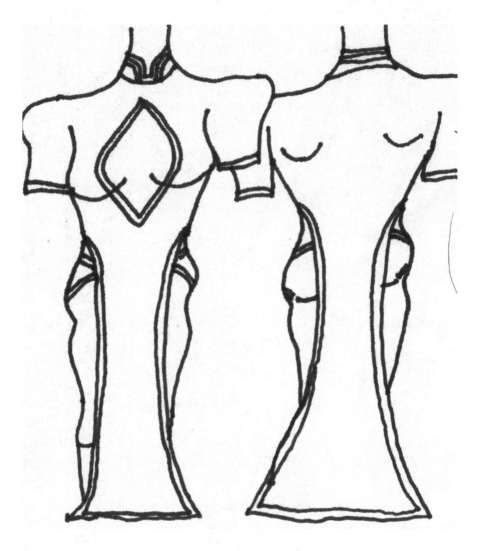

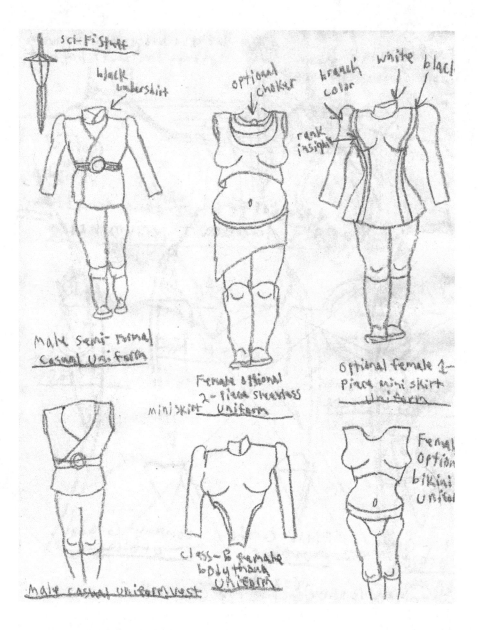

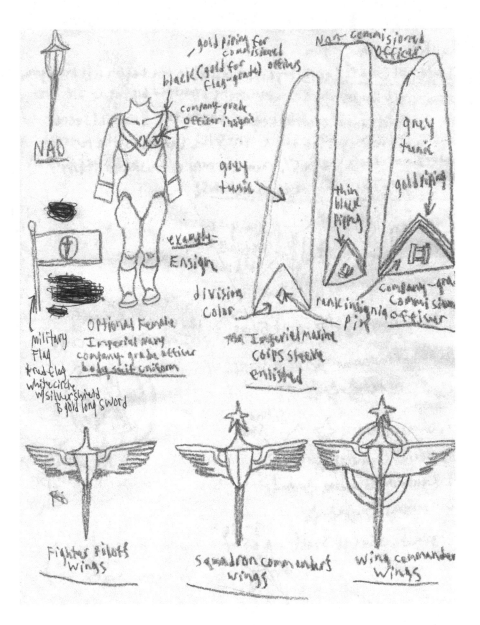

NAD

gold piping for
commissioned

black (gold for
Flag-grade) officers

company-grade
officer insignia

grey
tunic

Non commisioned
officer

grey
tunic

gold piping

thin
black
piping

rank insignia
pin

company-grade
Commisioned
officer

example-
Ensign

division
color

The Imperial Marine
Corps sleeve
enlisted

Military
Flag
Kred Flag
whitecircle
w/silver shield
& gold long sword

Optional Female
Imperial Navy
company-grade officer
body suit uniform

Fighter Pilots
wings

Squadron commander's
wings

Wing commander
Wings

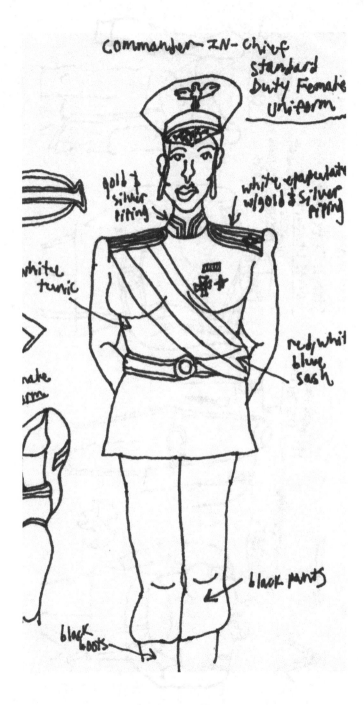

Commander-IN-Chief
Standard
Duty Female
Uniform

gold & silver piping

white epaulate w/gold & silver piping

white tunic

red/whit blue sash

black pants

black boots

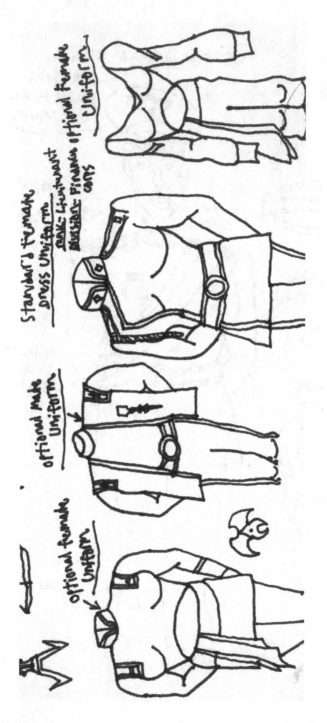

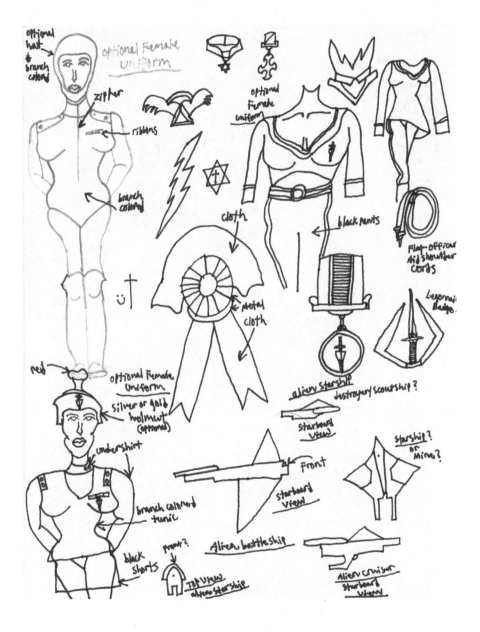

optional hat & branch colored

zipper

ribbons

optional Female uniform

optional Female uniform

branch colored

cloth

Metal cloth

black pants

Flag-Officer Aid shoulder cords

Legionnaire Badge

red

optional Female uniform

silver or gold helmut (optional)

undershirt

branch colored tunic

black shorts

alien starship destroyer/scoutship?

Starboard View

starship? or Mine?

front?

Front

Starboard View

Top View alien starship

Alien battleship

Alien cruiser Starboard View

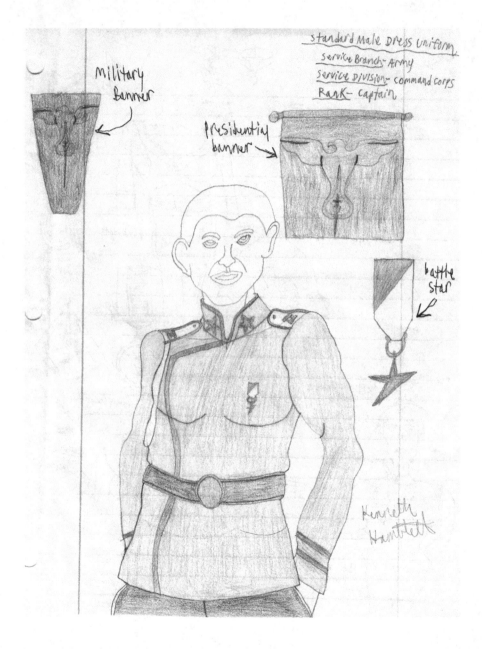

Military banner

Standard Male Dress Uniform
Service Branch- Army
Service Division- command corps
Rank- captain

Presidential banner

battle star

Kenneth Hamblett

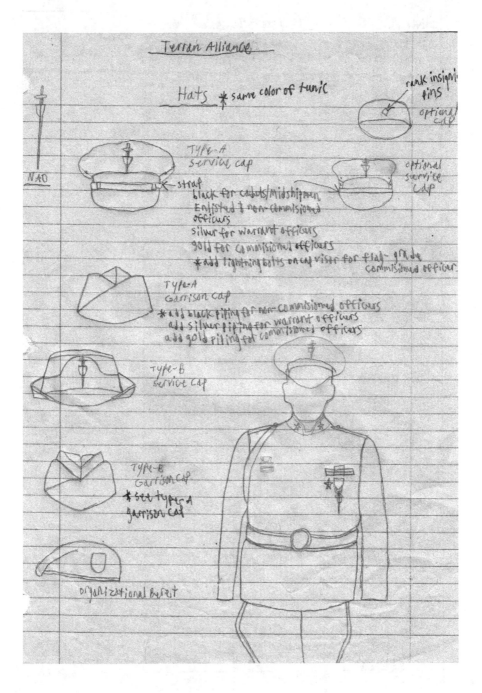

universe-
Star Battles

Terran Alliance

optional Female Uniform

rank- ensign branch- Imperial Navy

Kennith
Hamblett

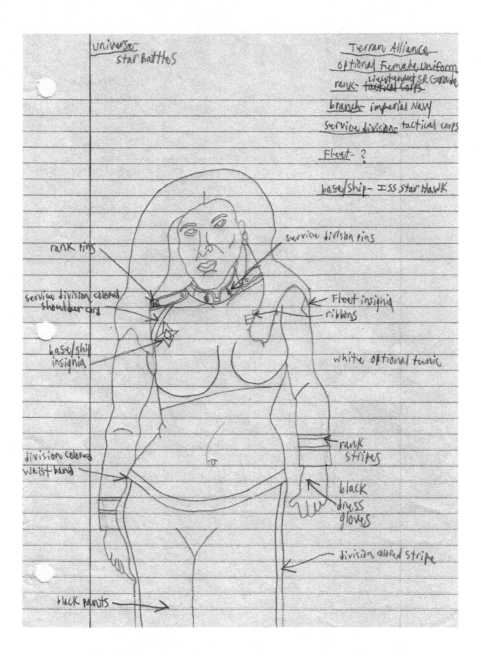

universe-
star battles

Terran Alliance
optional Female uniform
rank- lieutenant SR Grade tactical corps
branch- imperial Navy
service division- tactical corps

Fleet- ?

base/ship- ISS Star Hawk

rank pins

service division pins

service division colored shoulder cag

Fleet insignia ribbons

base/ship insignia

white optional tunic

rank stripes

division colored waist band

black dress gloves

division colored stripe

black pants

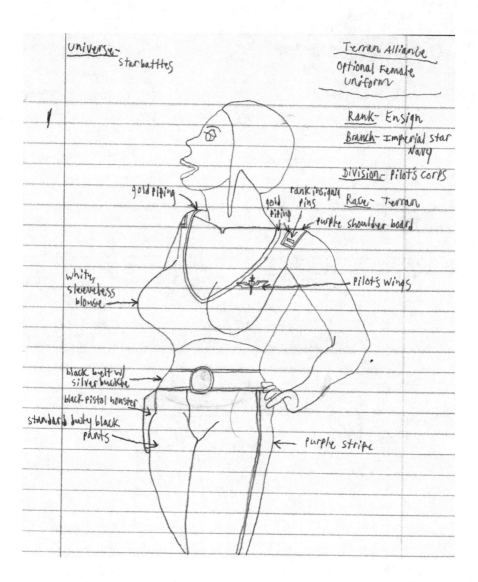

Universe ~
  Starbattles

Terran Alliance
Optional Female
Uniform

Rank ~ Ensign
Branch ~ Imperial star
            Navy
Division ~ Pilot's corps
Race ~ Terran

gold piping

gold piping

rank insignia pins

purple shoulder board

white sleeveless blouse ~

Pilot's wings

black belt w/ silver buckle

black pistol holster

standard duty black pants

purple stripe

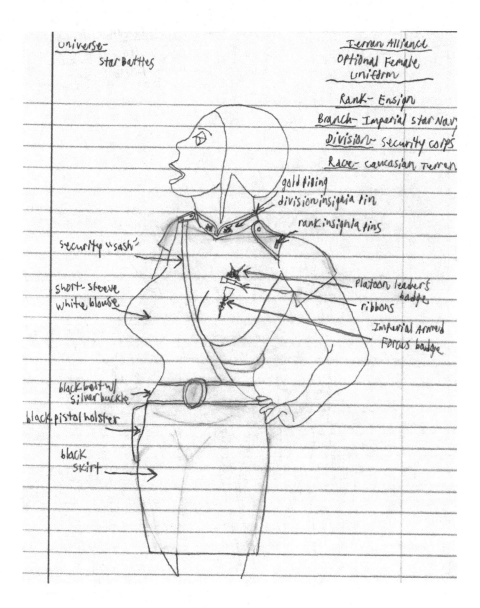

universe-
star battles

Terran Alliance
Optional Female
uniform

Rank- Ensign

Branch- Imperial star Navy

Division- security corps

Race- caucasian Terran

gold piling
division insignia pin
rank insignia pins

security "sash"

Platoon leader's badge

ribbons

Imperial Armed Forces badge

short-sleeve white blouse

black belt w/ silver buckle

black pistol holster

black skirt

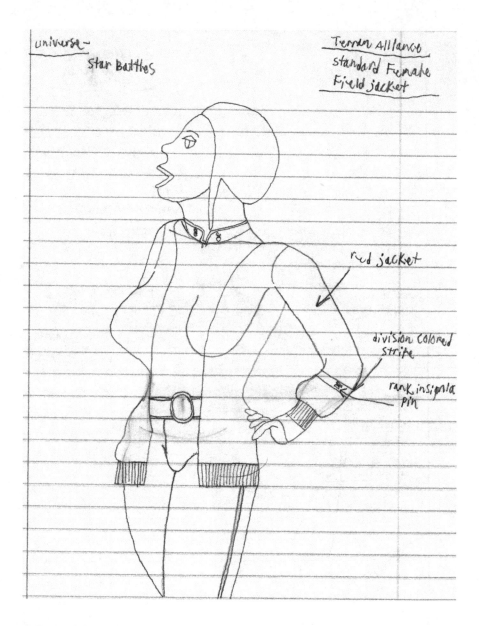

universe —
Star Battles

Terren Alliance
standard Female
Field jacket

red jacket

division colored
stripe

rank insignia
pin

universe-
　Star Battles

Terran Alliance
Standard Duty Female
　Uniform

Rank- commodore
Branch- Imperial Star
　　　　　Navy

Division- Medical Corps

Race- caucasian
　　　　Terran

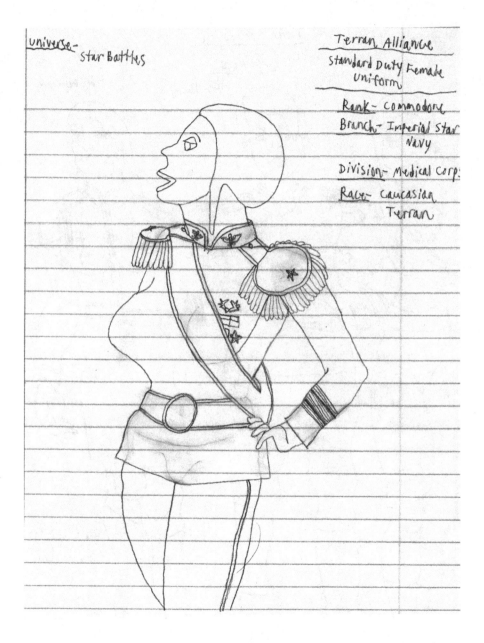

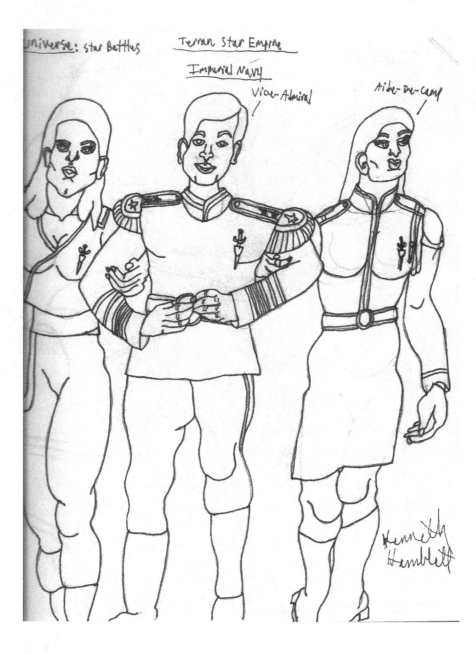

Universe: Star Battles

Terran Star Empire

Imperial Navy

Vice-Admiral

Aide-De-Camp